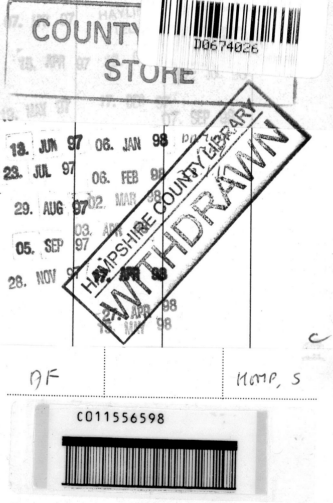

WHAT DREAD HAND?

WHAT DREAD HAND?

A Doctor Tina May Mystery Thriller

SARAH KEMP

CENTURY

LONDON MELBOURNE AUCKLAND JOHANNESBURG

Copyright © Sarah Kemp 1987

All rights reserved

First published in Great Britain in 1987 by
Century Hutchinson Ltd
Brookmount House, 62–65 Chandos Place
London WC2N 4NW

Century Hutchinson South Africa (Pty) Ltd
PO Box 337, Bergvlei, 2012 South Africa

Century Hutchinson Australia Pty Ltd
PO Box 496, 16–22 Church Street, Hawthorn
Victoria 3122, Australia

Century Hutchinson New Zealand Limited
PO Box 40-086, Glenfield, Auckland 10
New Zealand

ISBN 0 7126 1458 3

Photoset and printed in Great Britain by
WBC Print Ltd, Bristol

One

In August of that year, Tina May found she was unable to sleep well at night. Part of the trouble lay in her fear of the uneasy images that she was conjuring up in her dreams. For the first time in her life, she resorted to sleeping pills, and they seemed to iron out the images into imprecise, dark alleyways through which she was able to progress till she woke up with the dawn, a foul taste in her mouth and the beginnings of a headache. Pretty soon she packed up the pills.

Her TV presentation *The Pathologist* (Tina seldom referred to it as a 'show') was into its second series and still doing well in the ratings. Her forensic work, both private and public, continued to enhance her reputation and was a source of considerable job satisfaction; she had plenty of loving, giving friends; was better off financially than she had ever dreamed in her wildest imaginings; enjoyed basic good health (confirmed by a thorough medical check-up) – so why should she be falling apart so easily?

It was beginning to show in her appearance. Susan the make-up girl at the TV studios was the first to spot the tiredness around the eyes, the slight yellowing of skin.

'*Too many late nights, Tina.*' That was Susan's verdict.

Tina began to take the issue quite seriously when she almost – but not quite – dried up during one of her recordings. The silliest thing in the world: Toby Jakeman, acting as her interviewer-cum-feed, put a question about rigor mortis – how long it took to appear, how long the effect lasted, and so forth. She, who had the facts and figures, the fallacies and pitfalls, at her fingertips, fluffed the answer – not

1

once, but twice. In the hiatus before the second re-take, she heard director Gerry Hackett-Bryce quite clearly through the intercom:

'That's not like our Tina. Maybe it's time we rested her for a bit.'

It was after this session that she locked herself in the private loo which was her special perquisite for being a star, and unaccountably cried herself into a swollen-eyed orgy of self-pity, something she had not done since the time she was first stood up on a teenage date.

The dream sequence, that night, was particularly bad.

Two evenings after that, she kept a dinner date with Dermot Heymans – an event to which she had been looking forward with no great enthusiasm, for all that Heymans amused her when she was in the right sort of mood. He – though old enough to be her father – remained convinced that it was only a matter of time and pressure of personality before she succumbed to his seductive arts: Heymans was something of a showman, the clown of Harley Street, boulevardier and bon vivant, with the face and physique of an ageing medieval warlock – and, withal, a brilliant psychiatrist who had squandered his talents in the successful pursuit of wealth and a certain popular fame through the media.

Tina joined him at his favourite Soho restaurant, where the staff grovelled at his slightest beck and call. He bounced to his feet at her entry: tight-waisted in his double-breasted pin stripe, a red silk handkerchief fluttering like a battle flag in his breast pocket, diamond stick-pin in the black silk knitted tie that he always affected. ('In perpetual mourning for my lost innocence, darling.')

In the perverse way in which one so often takes more pains over one's appearance for people one likes least, Tina had actually gone out and bought a new dress for the occasion, and had spent a quite interminable time and trouble over her hair and make-up. Her efforts were well rewarded:

'My dear Tina – how very, very nice to see you. And even more beautiful than ever – if such a thing were possible!' This was delivered in his loud, corncrake voice which, together with the hand-kissing and the excessively theatrical production of settling her in her chair, provided the dinner-time clientele of the restaurant with a fair approximation to a cabaret. One had to put up with this kind of treatment from Heymans. Or simply do without him.

He ordered the meal with hardly any reference to his guest. This behaviour was all of a piece with his superficial gallantry: Heymans did not acknowledge the presence of women's liberation, and his ethic in the relationship between the sexes was fossilized somewhere around the year 1910. If married, he would almost certainly have referred to his spouse as 'the little woman'.

Having satisfied himself that – at his suggestion – Tina would wish to have Parma ham followed by Sweetbreads Financière, he launched into small-talk which, as usual, started off with a quiz about the doings of their mutual friends and acquaintances.

'Did you hear that Marc Struthers has been adopted for the by-election at Wormot – a safe seat if there ever was one? Isn't he greatly improved since his knighthood? More relaxed. An intensely ambitious man who can now comfortably set his sights on his next goal of attorney-general rewarded by a peerage.'

Yes, Tina had read about Marc standing for Parliament, but hadn't seen him since he received his accolade from the Queen. . . .

'And the estimable Arkwright has been promoted to Superintendent. A feather in the cap of Scotland Yard, that Arkwright. One hopes he goes all the way to the top.'

Yes, Tina had heard about Derek Arkwright's promotion; in fact he had lunched her in celebration. . . .

'That ex-husband of yours – have you managed to marry him off yet, Tina?'

Yes, she supposed so – but hadn't recieved an invitation to

3

the wedding, whenever it had been, and presumably up in Scotland. . . .

A pause – and then Heymans leaned forward and, in the inimitable way he had, replaced a comic mask with a serious mask, eyeing her very earnestly.

'My dear, I hope you won't think I'm prying,' he said, 'but I have the most distinct impression that something's preying on your mind. Speaking not as a psychiatrist, but as your friend, would you like to talk to me about it?'

Almost miraculously, his unbidden declaration opened up a floodgate in her mind. With no very great embarrassment, Tina found that she was beginning to tell him what had troubled her in the first instance and was still secretly troubling her, waking and sleeping – but mostly sleeping. . . .

CAMBRIDGE – 3. . . .

Three miles to go. Soon be there, thank God. A stiff gin and tonic followed by a bath, before going off to the dinner.

Tina didn't like driving after dark, especially in winter. Come to think of it, she didn't like driving – period. No car of her own; used taxis in London, and hired anything going from her local garage for any out-of-town trips that she didn't make by train.

A thin wraith of mist drifted across her front, coming from right to left on the easterly wind from the fens. She automatically checked her speed – unlike the driver of the juggernaut who had been aching to pass her ever since the Bishop's Stortford turn-off; he pulled out into the centre, lane, lights winking; she felt the buffeting of his slipstream against the light body of her Mini as he swept past, cut across her front end and was gone into the night with his battery of blood-red rear lights staring back at her.

She switched on the radio for the news items: the oily voice of the announcer informed her that the latest East–West summit meeting was closing with the predictable absence of accord, and that a woman had given live birth to sextuplets in

4

Wisconsin. A man was helping the Hertfordshire police in connection with the missing schoolgirl. . . .

The bank of fog hit her with almost physical force.

One instant, she could see the painted white lines as clearly as if they had been etched in coloured acid on the dark road; next, they had gone and in their place was a world of dirty grey cotton wool that was all around her, and, sucked up by the air conditioning, was even filling the inside of the little car.

She stabbed her foot on the brake – and then realized with a simultaneous shock of alarm that she had no idea if anyone was close behind her or not. She thought not – but something could have crept up quickly while her attention was upon the overtaking juggernaut. . . .

She cut in closer to the verge. To her utter relief, the broad white line marking its presence made a shifting appearance there through the crawling murk. All she had to do was to keep both her eyes to the front, mark the verge out of the corner of one eye, drive at a speed commensurate with her range of vision (which wasn't much), and pray that she didn't overshoot the Cambridge turn-off, which should come up any moment now.

The news announcer declared that there was widespread fog in the Midlands and East Anglia. . . .

Thanks for the information, chum! She snapped it off.

Then came the fire!

Its first manifestation was a faint pinkness of the fog ahead, which, before she had time to make a true appreciation of the possible cause, blossomed into a full redness, took shape, dimension, scale – all of it terrifying.

Next, before her vision had encompassed that and spelt the message to her brain, the mechanism of sight/appreciation/reaction was given another problem – a scene comprised of black shapes of indeterminate size and outline silhouetted against what she now accepted as fire.

Immediately after, she appreciated the size and shape of a juggernaut lying on its side and *facing* her!

Beyond that, two more shapes.

And some figures: curiously elongated in the unearthly light.

Stamping hard down on the brake, she swung the wheel verge-wise. As she went over the white line and slammed into the foot of the grassy slope beyond, another car streaked past, overtaking her with its horn blaring. From the corner of her eye, she saw it smash straight into the front of the overturned juggernaut. Its horn went silent.

When she clambered out of the Mini, the full horror of the situation hit her: sound, vision and smell. Someone was shrieking – a man; flitting figures were lit up in the hellish glare of the flames; and the stink of burning rubber permeated everything.

She ran forward – towards the burly figure of a man in overalls, who looked as if he might have been the driver of the juggernaut.

'I'm a doctor!' she called out. 'Is anyone hurt?'

'You gotter be joking, lady!' came the bawled response. 'What's needed 'ere is a bleeding hearse!'

He was standing in the middle of the slow lane, his face – quite nice-looking in a beefy, bovine kind of way – was a mask of frightened irresolution, and there was a cut across his brow that trailed a pattern of blood down one cheek. He turned away and walked slowly towards the front of the juggernaut, where the newly-arrived car had buried itself half-way under the big driver's cab, so that only its pathetic rear end was showing; the front part seemed to have become telescoped and flattened almost to nothing. No one could possibly have been alive inside there; nor did the trucker make any attempt to look and see; he groped vaguely inside the open door of his cab and, appearing not to find what he sought, leaned against the bodywork and gave way to a paroxysm of sobbing.

More cars were arriving on the scene, as she – Tina – went forward towards the source of the conflagration, where the man was screaming.

There was a motor coach on fire: flame and thick diesel

6

smoke blotting it out. Its windows and doors were open and the gaunt figures who stood around must have been its passengers, miraculously all escaped. A jumble of three cars was piled up beside the coach, and an elderly man was being helped out of the rear passengers' seat of one which lay on its side: he was the screamer, his face a mask of blood. They were clearing the second car in the pile-up; Tina saw at a glance that its driver's head was protruding out of the shattered windscreen; the man was part-decapitated and quite dead.

'Give us a hand, miss,' said a fellow who was trying to extricate a young man from the driving seat of the third car, who was half-in, half-out, and jerking his right leg, which appeared to be jammed somewhere inside the workings of the vehicle.

Tina joined the helper who was trying to pull the other free.

'Don't worry, chum, we'll soon have you out of there!' said the helper.

'Yeah! – thassright,' muttered the other, gritting his teeth. 'Got it stuck somewhere under the wheel when it collapsed. Silly, really.'

'One – two – three –' intoned Tina's companion to her. 'And he-e-eave!' They pulled together, the victim straining also.

'And again! . . .'

It was then that the car nearest to the burning coach also ignited with a muffled blast that scorched Tina's cheek. It was almost immediately joined by the vehicle with the near-headless corpse in the driving seat.

'Get me outa here!' cried their young man to his helpers, as he bucked and reared and fought against his imprisoned leg. '*I'm gonna be next!*'

His panic communicated itself to Tina and her companion; they fought and scrabbled to drag him clear, while the flames from the next car licked the paintwork inches from where they stood, and heat grew more intense by the passing second.

'He's stuck – really stuck!' breathed the man by her side.

There was no need for him to keep his voice down; the victim was as well aware as they – more so – of the hazard in which he lay. He had begun to keen quietly, whilst still jerking at his leg.

And then Tina remembered that, against all likelihood, she had her instrument case in the Mini's boot (left over from yesterday, when she had first hired the car to attend a panic post mortem in Surrey; and who would take forensic surgical instruments to a dinner and seminar in Cambridge – except by an oversight?)

'Hey! Where are you going?' cried her companion-helper, as she relinquished her hold on the victim's shoulder and turned to run.

'I'll be back!' she shouted.

The Mini's boot was locked. She dived into the car, snatched the bunch of keys from the ignition. Opened up the door of the boot. The instrument case lay under her weekend valise. Well under. When she picked it up, the lid flew open and the contents were spread over the dark bottom of the tiny compartment. Sobbing, now, with frustration added to anguish, she scrabbled for the things she wanted: a large scalpel and a pair of shears which would cut through bone like cheese.

She had them both in hand, and was running back to the car, when it exploded into a fireball like the rest.

The searingly hot blast met her; stopped her dead.

Her late helper was staggering back, hands over her face, his hair alight and forming a curious halo about his head.

The man in the driver's seat of the car – the victim – was quite unscathed, for the genesis of the blaze had taken place outside the body work. He was untouched – for the present.

Tina saw her way clear to amputating the fateful leg in seconds.

Bowing her head against the intense heat, she went forward. . . .

And stopped in her tracks three paces from her goal – when

she felt her skin begin to singe, and distinctly caught an acrid stink that could only have been her woollen car-coat beginning to burn.

The victim's hands were stretched out to her in a gesture of agonized entreaty.

She fought with her mind to advance her foot – but nothing happened.

She shook her head at the man in the car.

And then – he began to scream. And Tina May screamed in return.

The sounds – his and hers – which had haunted her dreams and made hideous her days ever since, were not stilled till the consuming fire imploded into the car and turned the writhing body of the victim into charred bone and black ash in less time than it takes to tell.

Her dreadful story told, Tina relaxed in her seat and looked down at her hands which, surprisingly, betrayed by not so much as a tremor the way she felt.

Heymans had been splendid throughout her telling of the appalling episode: neither interrupting, nor calling attention to them both by visible display of horror, compassion, distaste. It seemed that, as far as the rest of the clientele and the staff of the restaurant were concerned, Tina might just as well have been recounting the tale of a particularly tedious cocktail party she had attended.

'And I've dreamed about it every night since,' she said. 'And almost without trying, I can see that man's face when he began to roast.

'But – most of all – it's the screaming that disturbs me most. Both of us, you see? Mine as well as his. . . .'

'It puzzles you – that you should still be living with it?' asked Heymans.

She nodded. 'I deal with death all the time,' she said. 'And in its ugliest forms, much of the time. Traffic accident victims. Burnings. The violently-dead. The long-dead.' She looked up

9

to face him. 'Why should this one have cracked me up so badly, Dermot? Tell me that.'

'My dear,' he said, 'in your particular persuasion, you deal with the *fact* of death, not the *dying* of it. I've heard you say – several times – that you chose to be what you humorously describe as a "corpse doctor". . . .'

'Not my term, that isn't!' she interposed. 'My friends of the *Sunday Courier* dreamed up the "corpse doctor" tag, but thank heaven it's never really caught on. Sorry to cut in on you – please don't stop.'

Heymans may have been a good listener; he also did not like being interrupted, and showed it by a slight pursing of the lips. 'As I was saying,' he continued, 'you chose to be a forensic pathologist because, despite all your brains and talents, you couldn't guarantee to keep every patient alive for ever – and that was your entire need as a physician.'

She nodded. 'You're right,' she said. 'I hate the whole concept of dying and its appurtenances – like graveyards. Do you know, Dermot, the only thing I hate about my job is when I have to attend at some dreadful cemetery at an unearthly hour of the morning to supervise an exhumation? You see – I do face up to my shortcomings, and that's psychologically healthy, isn't it?'

Heymans took up his glass of crème de menthe and deliberately sipped at it before replying; when he did, his puckish, boot-button black eyes sought her out challengingly.

'Did you ever face up to Johnny Kettle dying, Tina?' he asked.

At the mention of a man who had been her father, brother, mentor, teacher, inspiration, and a lot else, Tina closed her eyes.

'That wasn't fair,' she whispered. 'That was below the belt.'

'Life – and death – are also below the belt, my dear,' he replied. 'When Kettle died, there was nothing you could do to stop it – so, in a sense, you made it into a non-happening. You wouldn't let yourself grieve – not beyond the outward

10

observances that self-respect and convention demand. To let yourself grieve *inside* would have been a form of acceptance and acknowledgement of his death. Of the physical act of his dying.'

'And so? . . .' She stared at him challengingly.

'And so, you have set up a situation whereby your mind – and the mind is a very subtle, fine-tuned instrument, Tina, which is not to be circumvented or short-changed – has avenged itself on you by having its own way in the end.'

'What *do* you mean?' she asked, prejudiced against his mysterious discipline – now that it was directed against her – as any layman.

'I mean, my dear Tina, that when Johnny Kettle died and there was nothing you could do to prevent it, you wouldn't let yourself grieve because grief for the dead is a form of acceptance and acknowledgement of the inevitable act.

'What you are doing now is working through your grief for Johnny by means of a substitute whose dying was brought to your notice in a particularly brutal and graphic manner that you were unable to cram down into your subconscious.

'You are working out your grief for Johnny through the death of a total stranger!'

'So what am I to do about it – do I just suffer till it goes away?'

They had gone back to his elegant Georgian town house in Harley Street, just around the corner from his exclusive clinic. Soft-footed on the priceless Isfahan rugs, Heymans was serving Turkish coffee and brandy. *The Four Seasons* discreetly seeped out of the hi-fi and permeated the room.

'Whatever happens, you don't fight it, Tina. Ideally, you should go away somewhere and work it through. A complete change of ambience. New faces. New friends. Fresh aspirations. Then wait for the mind to relent and let you off the hook. You would find, incidentally, that you might get around to shedding a few entirely healthy tears for Johnny. And that would be therapeutically beneficial.'

'I had in mind for a week in Brittany before my new series starts next month,' she said. 'But I've done nothing about it. Not even given any thought about who's going to feed the cat while I'm away.'

Heymans smiled. 'Do nothing in a hurry,' he said. 'Merely direct your mind to the notion of spending what's left of the summer away from it all. Somewhere quiet. Peaceful. Let the mind absorb the idea. It will do the rest.'

Tina raised an eyebrow at that. 'Dermot, I don't *think* that I'm quite so much the slave of my mind's whims as you seem to imagine,' she said. 'Not to go running off into the long grass for the rest of the summer upon a mere caprice.'

He nodded archly and switched to his comic mask. 'Oh, I know you to be a very strong-willed lady,' he said. 'Make no mistake about that. Just tolerate the notion of capriciousness with a certain benevolence and let a little time go by.

'Oh, and by the way, I know just the place for you to go.'

'Where's that?' asked Tina.

'Give me a ring when you've made up your mind,' he replied. Nor was he to be drawn any further.

The dinner with Dermot Heymans was on a Tuesday. The following Monday Tina was called upon at short notice to carry out a post mortem at the South-West mortuary. The subject, a young woman of twenty-three, had been 'larking around' with her boyfriend (the very term used by him) in the kitchenette of the flat they shared in Croydon, when the kitchen knife which she was holding during a make-believe fight over who was to lay the table resulted in the point of the knife entering her chest and penetrating the heart, causing instantaneous death.

The issue seemed fairly straightforward: a matter of a routine coroner's verdict of 'accidental death' or possibly 'death through misadventure'; except that Tina was unable to account, in her own mind, for a small cut on the palm of the

12

woman's left hand, which, though slight, had the look of a defensive wound.

If, as the boyfriend had attested, the couple had had a friendly, laughing struggle, in the course of which his partner had inadvertently turned the knife against herself, so that the point had penetrated between her ribs during mutual contact of their bodies, why had she sustained a cut on the hand in the process of trying to prevent it?

The young detective sergeant who was handling the case and who attended the post mortem was quite impressed by Tina's finding. Perhaps he visualized himself as the impresario of a major cause célèbre. In any event, he made careful note of her report and resolved to probe more deeply into the relationship between the dead woman and her companion. And to keep Tina informed.

It was past six o'clock in the evening before Tina had cleaned up, changed and summoned a taxi back to Lochiel Street, Chelsea, where her cat, You by name, was certain to be awaiting his supper with unconcealed impatience. The sky was heavily overcast and threatening rain when she reached home, and she had scarcely paid off the cab when she noticed to her slight annoyance that she had left a light burning in the upstairs sitting room – which was inexplicable, because it had been bright sunshine when she had left the house after lunch. Very odd, she thought.

The mystery deepened when, after letting herself in, she found You the cat fast asleep in his basket, having got in through the cat-flap on the garden door. He opened one eye to regard her, licked his lips and went back to sleep again. Tina was puzzling over his bowl, which was lying on the floor, licked clean, but still bearing the heavy and all-pervasive odour of his favourite tinned cat food, when the light tread of footfalls descending the stairs triggered off her adrenaline.

'Who's there?' she called out.

'Tina – it's me!'

And in through the door walked a familiar figure: her former secretary-cum-companion, whom she had last seen some five months previously when the latter had left for Scotland.

'Maggie!' exclaimed Tina. 'What are *you* doing here?'

'I let myself in,' said the other, adding irrelevantly: 'I still have my key.'

'Is Jock with you?'

(Jock being Tina's ex-husband, to whom Maggie had flown, and who – blessedly – she had taken unto herself, thereby freeing Tina of the intolerable burden of his continued presence.)

'No, Tina,' replied Maggie. 'He – he's left me.'

It was ironic, not to say macabre, to be comforting someone for being deserted by one's former husband – even if she was still nominally a friend. Tina's capacity for calm acceptance, aided by her sense of humour, helped her to handle the crisis. This she did in the good old traditional British way of first making them both a nice cup of tea, having done which, she got down to the facts of the case.

'Why did he go, Maggie?' she asked.

'He – he had one of his wonderful opportunities,' replied the other, dabbing her nose with Tina's handkerchief.

'Oh!' responded Tina, who thought she saw it all. 'And what's the current wonderful opportunity, pray?'

The last time, it had been a foolproof, copper-bottomed scheme to provide some colour for the lonely crews of North Sea offshore oil rigs in the form of live entertainment – notably girls – girls – girls. This enterprise had got no further than a brusque refusal at the head office of the oil company, following upon which, Jock had assaulted the executive in question and had been bound over to keep the peace for twelve months. Before that, the wonderful opportunity had been – well, Tina had quite forgotten. In the years she had known Jock, in and out of marriage, he had never come to accept the notion of making a fairly comfortable living by his quite considerable competence as a writer; no, there was

14

nothing for it but that he must be a millionaire overnight. It was all very sad.

'He came home late one night,' said Maggie, 'with this story about having met a chap at the club. . . .'

'Oh, those chaps at the club,' said Tina. 'Or at the pub, or the races, or at an Old Boys' reunion dinner – sorry – please go on.'

Jock's get-rich-quick schemes generally followed a fairly predictable pattern; this latest one had at least the virtues of a certain originality. The chap at the club was an Australian, who was imminently returning there in order to take formal possession of a small island off the north-east of the antipodean continent which was as yet unclaimed by any other power or authority; and there set up an international merchant banking consortium specializing in offshore deals, along with the kind of fringe facilities that would put Zurich in the shade. And the beauty of the scheme – as Jock had explained to Maggie in the dark hours of the night after his return from the club – was that it called for a minimum of personal capital; the rest of the money would be sucked in.
' "Sucked in" – that was the actual term he used.'

'How much personal capital?' asked Tina, who had been this way many times before.

Maggie mentioned a figure: it comprised her personal savings, plus what she had been able to persuade the bank to lend her. Armed with that, Jock had departed to Australia the previous Monday. She had not heard if he had arrived safely.

'You'll see him again when the money's run out and his partner has probably gone with it,' predicted Tina. 'The best thing for you, my dear, is to bite on a bullet, wait for the statutory three years to pass, and then divorce him. Believe me, he'll never change.'

This caused Maggie to look at her in some surprise. 'Oh, we never got around to marrying,' she said. 'Didn't I write and tell you?'

Tina shook her head in amazement, and then in wry

15

acceptance. 'Well, then you've got nothing to worry about,' she said. 'You can have your job back here, because I've missed you very much, and. . . .

'Why are you looking at me like that, Maggie?'

Maggie Wainwright's large and lustrous eyes – features that lifted her by far from out of the common ruck of the average *jolie laide* – were swimming with tears again.

'Tina,' she faltered, 'you'll probably change your mind when you hear that – that I'm pregnant.'

Tina by no means changed her mind.

She supposed she had always known, deep down, that there was never to be any ridding herself of Jock Hardacre, and that by relinquishing Maggie Wainwright to his care she was not losing an ex-husband so much as taking on a surrogate sister-in-law. And so it had transpired – save that there was also to be a surrogate sister-in-law's baby to make up the trio.

That night, her sleep was unusually free of the disturbing images that had bedevilled her since the motorway tragedy, and she put it down to a certain promise of a solution that had come her way since the ad hoc psychoanalysis she had received from Dermot Heymans a few days previously. Obedient to his advice, she had let the idea of taking a protracted rest marinate quietly in her subconscious – while all the time telling herself that there was no chance at all of walking out of the house and leaving everything – her career and the voluminous correspondence that went with it, not to mention You the cat and everything else – at a moment's notice.

But now. . . .

She had Maggie back again! And that changed everything!

Tina telephoned Heymans at his clinic that same morning and was answered by the matron, a starchy lady who for

16

reasons best known to herself disapproved of Tina May and all her works and took no great trouble to hide the fact.

No, Doctor Heymans was not available, she informed Tina, but he had been expecting to hear from Doctor May and had given instructions for the details of the Cornish cottage to be dispatched to Doctor May as soon as she telephoned.

What Cornish cottage? Why, the cottage that Doctor Heymans owned in Cornwall, naturally. And with that, she rang off.

The brochure arrived in a large envelope at 18 Lochiel Street by the next post. Put out by a famous West End firm of estate agents, it pictured a 'dream' country cottage of stone, with a stone-tiled roof in the Cornish manner; roses round the door, leaded window panes and stone mullions over, bargeboard front door open to reveal tantalizing hints of a wealth of oak beams; and a riotous surround of lupins, snapdragons, hollyhocks and the like. One could almost hear the bees humming.

The details were equally enticing:

CLIFFTOP COTTAGE
Trepoll Haven,
nr St Costello,
S. Cornwall.

A charming period cottage lovingly modernized by the present owner, yet totally unspoilt. Situated at the end of a private road from Trepoll village and its abundant amenities, yet perfectly isolated, with views of the breathtaking coastline and 1 minute from the sandy beach. Individual artist's paintings a special feature. ACCOMMODATION: 2 double bedrooms, lounge, study, solarium, fully equipped kitchen, bathroom en suite, shower cabinet, 3 working open fireplaces. Solid fuel stove + immersion heater. To let, fully-furnished. . . .

There was a lot more, ending with a price which had been

17

scratched out and replaced by a note in Heymans' sprawled handwriting:

Tina, darling – The place is yours till the schools begin again in September, the point being that I don't allow ghastly children at my lovely retreat. I have a childless old couple moving in on September 19th. The cottage is yours till then – free, gratis and for nothing – and with all my love, D.H.

There still remained the question of whether Simon Elles and Gerald Hackett-Bryce, producer and director respectively of *The Pathologist*, would put up with the idea of her absenting herself for weeks on end before the new series started up the following month. The publicity people would inevitably require personal appearances, both live and in the TV and radio media, press interviews, and so forth, to blazon the show – the presentation.

She tackled Elles over luncheon the following day. He took her to the Savoy and was his usual bland, smooth and attentive self.

'The ratings having held for the first two series,' he said, 'I see no reason why the third shouldn't also break all records in its particular line. And the publicity and PR crowd are with me in this.'

Tina, toying with a plain grilled sole, decided to tackle the issue of her 'retreat' obliquely:

'Simon,' she said, 'do you think it would be possible to schedule the publicity and PR stunts so that they were all recorded over a period of – say – two or three days?'

'Why's that?' he asked.

'Well, I'm thinking of taking off to darkest Cornwall for the rest of the summer – well, till the end of August – and, frankly, the prospect of being summoned up to London at a moment's notice to do a spot on a magazine programe or a chat show will rather defeat the object of the exercise – which is to get a little peace and quiet. As for personal appearances – I'd much prefer to give the opening of garden parties syndrome a miss this time round. . . .'

'Say no more, darling, say no more,' interposed Elles, smiling and laying a reassuring hand on hers. 'One day, alone, will do for the publicity clips. And we'll schedule that at your entire convenience. As for the garden party syndrome – pfui! – we can leave all that stuff till you come back from your holiday in September and the show's doing very nicely thank you.

'So how's that?' He gave her hand a squeeze.

Tina, who had been expecting, if not a fight, at least a protracted skirmish to get her own way, was hugely delighted with the outcome. And yet – oddly – there sprang up in her mind a nagging, niggling thought that it had maybe been a victory *too* easily won. Should not Simon have fought a little harder to have the star of his show at his beck and call, to be thrown into the firing line whenever and for whatever reason there appeared an opportunity to boost *The Pathologist*?

Her pondering was interrupted by Elles waving at someone across the room, and then half-rising. . . .

'Tina, here's your chum Jeremy Cook and his bride,' he murmured.

'Jeremy and Jessica – how nice. . . .'

Jeremy was a former close friend who had 'married well' – as the carpers, cavillers and quibblers were fond of reiterating. In fact, Jessica was six or seven years older than he, and rich in her own right. Tina had not seen either of them since their wedding at St Margaret's, Westminster – but she only had to take one look at them to know that they were both quite blatantly happy.

She and Jessica kissed.

'Tina, you must come and stay with us,' said the other. 'We've bought the dearest summer house on the Thames, with a little boat to go with it.'

'A break will do you the world of good, duckie,' said Jeremy, kissing her in his usual brotherly manner. 'You look as if you need a change and a rest.'

'Dear me,' said Tina when they had gone. 'Do I really look as if I'm about to slip into a decline, like the heroine of some Victorian melodrama? Am I interestingly pale? Have I developed a slight cough that's escaped my notice?'

Elles laughed lightly, but it seemed to her that he pointedly avoided her eye.

'Oh, we all have our good days and our not-so-good days, Tina,' he said. 'And you really have been marvellous. To have done two series straight off – *and* two episodes of the third already in the can. It's bound to tell on one. I'm not one bit surprised that you've decided to let everything go hang and buzz off to darkest Cornwall for the rest of the summer.' He reached out across the table and squeezed her hand comfortingly. 'And you can rely on me, darling – and Gerald, and the rest of the boys and girls of the old firm – to rally round and back you up through thick and thin.

'Thick and thin!'

'Thank you, Simon,' responded Tina, somewhat bemused.

After all, the declaration – though undoubtedly sincere, and transparently well meant – did rather sound like the sort of reassurance one gives to brave young airmen departing on suicide missions over enemy territory, or to people who take to their bed with a terminal illness, and everyone in the know about it but themselves.

She studied herself in the bathroom mirror that night.

'Am I really cracking up?' she asked herself. 'Have I really been overdoing it? Taking the pitcher to the well once too often?

'And does it show?

'Jeremy and Jessica think so. Simon does, too.

'Dermot Heymans as good as hinted that I was on the way to some kind of nervous breakdown. *And* he's letting me have his Cornish cottage for free – and he with a reputation for meanness that's the talk of Harley Street.'

She ran her fingertips over her cheeks, the corners of her

20

eyes (and, surely, they were crepey and slack, where once they had been taut and firm).

'Well, thank God, I've caught it in time,' she concluded, much cheered by the idea. 'My holiday's sure to do me good, to give me a sound mind in a healthy body. And I'll come back to the fray – a new woman!'

Two

Tina packed everything she was likely to need in an old cabin trunk that she bought second-hand in the Portobello Road, and booked a seat to Cornwall by Great Western Railway. Once in Trepoll Haven, she told herself, she would restrict her movements between the cottage, the shops in the village, and the beach. And walk everywhere.

On the following Saturday afternoon, she was curled up in a window seat of a first-class compartment, a copy of her favourite Dickens on her lap and a glass of gin and tonic at her elbow; watching the estuary of the River Exe roll past like the backdrop to a model railway lay-out: with toy yachts reflected from glassy water, toy houses on the far shore, model animals set out in painted fields, and cotton wool clouds scumbled over a cobalt blue sky.

The departure from London had been quite painless. Indeed, Maggie had seemed delighted with the prospect of a safe and solitary haven back in her beloved Lochiel Street, with a not too demanding job to do, and a labour-saving small house in which to play chatelaine with the aid of a twice-weekly cleaning woman. Safely beyond the third month of her pregnancy, she was settling down to enjoy an experience which, like so many women, she found to be very much to her taste.

Almost the last thing before Tina's departure – with the taxi waiting at the door – she had a call from the South-West police station. It was the detective sergeant telling her that, following upon her findings at the post mortem on the stabbed woman, he had probed more deeply into the former life style of the couple – Angela Stewart and James Holmes by

22

name. It appeared that the neighbours had made frequent complaints about the rows that took place in the flat, and the landlord had several times threatened to evict the pair of them for non-payment of rent: Holmes was unemployed and Stewart had supported them both from her earnings as a cinema usherette.

But the most significant item he had turned up, said Detective Sergeant Vance, was that Holmes had been cheating Angela Stewart while she was still alive – and with not one, but two other women.

He would keep Doctor May informed, he said smugly. There was certainly more to the case than had appeared at first sight.

The episode unaccountably depressed Tina, who thought she saw in it the makings of a witch hunt – and perhaps all unwarranted; set in train by a hunch she had had about the small wound on the dead woman's hand. She had not given Vance (or anyone else, for that matter) the phone number of the Trepoll Haven cottage; Maggie had instructions to take all messages and relay to her only those which she considered to be important. One of the many good things about Maggie as a secretary: she had an admirable nose for distinguishing the essentials from the non-essentials.

Shutting her mind to all this, Tina addressed herself for the umpteenth time to the thorny path trodden by Sydney Carton on his lonely odyssey to the guillotine; time passed quickly as she sped through the fat landscape of Devon and Cornwall.

'St Costello – St Costello! The train is now arriving at St Costello!' The announcement came over the intercom. Tina closed her book and picked up her hand luggage.

'Sufferin' Jesus!'
The cry of the station taxi driver, who had obligingly offered to carry her cabin trunk into the cottage, alerted Tina to the fact – till then unnoticed by her – that she must be

living right on the edge of her nerve ends. She gave a start, felt her heart skip a beat, and found her lower lip to be trembling treacherously.

'What is it?' she cried, following the man in through the front door, and noticing that his wide-eyed stare was directed to something in the gloomy far end of the living room.

'Oh, good heavens!' she herself exclaimed. 'How simply – *awful!*'

The thing that confronted them from the surface of the whitewashed wall was recklessly foreshortened so as to give the appearance of actually flying *into* the room, through the wall, from somewhere beyond.

It was the figure of a man – or something resembling a man.

Goat-faced, grimacing, be-horned, with pale and malevolent goatish eyes – the classic representation of the Devil from time immemorial, it was making an intrusion into the cottage through that wall: punching its way in by means of its extended fist, which, again, was cunningly foreshortened to give the impression of actually probing far across the room and almost touching the viewer. Twice life-sized, or more, it was an extraordinarily skilful piece of *trompe-l'oeil* painting of the very highest order: conceived and executed, surely, by a hand that had been directed by a mind of a sick and perverted brilliance.

'Strewth, I be damned if I'd want to live alonger that thing!' declared the taxi driver, relieving himself of his burden, snatching up his fare, and making himself scarce.

The sound of the taxi bump-bumping over the rutted lane faded away into a near silence that was broken only by the far-off crash of Atlantic breakers on the beach below the cliff. Tina shivered and looked about her – carefully avoiding the sight of the figure painted on the end wall.

The room was furnished with good early Victorian pieces, along with some blue and white china, a few framed prints, and a portrait in oils over the open stone fireplace of a gentleman in a tall hat. All very Dermot Heymans – the representation of the Devil excepted.

She saw an envelope on a pretty marquetry table by one of the chintz-covered armchairs set each side of the fireplace. It was addressed to her. She opened and read it:

Tina, darling,
Welcome to my petit berceau, which I trust will be a peaceful arbour where you will find yourself again.

My most devastated apologies for the truly appalling (though tremendously clever) murals, which were painted for me, in lieu of payment for my services, by a patient, a very bad schizophrenic, who afterwards killed himself. I haven't yet found the heart to have them painted over. Believe me, if you have nothing better to do one wet afternoon, Tina, you have my blessing to slop some whitewash over them!

Overleaf is a list of useful local people, from the village copper to the man who will come and clear out your drains at a moment's notice, day or night.

Do drop me a postcard some time to let me know how you are faring.

   Lots of love,
    D.H.

Not mural – but *murals*! The thought of meeting up with more of the mad artist's horrendous work was almost too much, though at least there was the consolation of knowing what to expect: no more shocks out of the blue. She decided to look around the cottage immediately and learn the worst.

The lounge, or living room, occupied most of the front part of the building, and there were two doors leading off inside: one of them to the rear of the cottage. She tried the other one, which led into a small study, facing the front. It was furnished with a desk, office chair, bookshelves and bookcases, an easy chair – and another mural. . . .

This one showed some kind of human sacrifice. A nude woman stretched out on an altar was about to be slaughtered by the self-same devilish creature depicted in the living room. He was posed with a curved knife raised on high above the intended sacrifice, who lay there in wide-eyed terror, lips parted in a soundless scream.

Fortunately, one of the bookcases, easily movable and containing only a dozen or so paperbacks, was easy to drag across the room, to stand up against the mural so that it covered up the worst of the horror.

That done, Tina went to explore the rest of the ground floor. There was a short passage leading to a back door that opened out on to a glass lean-to which she supposed to be what the estate agent had described as a solarium. In the passage there were also doors leading to left and right, and a staircase to the right.

Beyond the right-hand door was a neat kitchen fitted with pine cupboards, cooker, washing machine, spin dryer, sink disposal unit and a large solid-fuel boiler. Happily, there was no room for a mural!

Not so the bathroom, which was across the passage. This had formerly been blessed with three blank walls – but no longer. The demonic artist had painted a seascape peopled with semi-nude figures swirling in and out of boisterous waves that lashed amongst offshore rocks and the fringe of a sandy beach. The creatures – nymphs, naiads, mermaids, satyrs and mermen – had the same leering, evil expressions as the diabolical creature shown elsewhere. Nevertheless the general effect was lighter, gayer and more acceptable than the other two murals.

So much for the work of the mad artist. The remainder of the cottage was quite bland and delightful. The upstairs bedrooms and shower room were simply and tastefully furnished. All the windows looked out on to breathtaking views of sea and clifftop, the slope leading down to the stone roofs of the village and the sleepy church tower, the haven and the boats.

Tina went back down to the solarium, which had a door that led out to a small garden set right on the cliff edge, with scarcely a couple of feet to spare beyond its fence before a sheer drop down to tumbled rocks and stark white sand.

There were several people walking the shoreline, all well wrapped up, because the wind was boisterous and the incoming breakers dangerous-looking. Quite close inshore a sailing boat was clawing its way into the eye of the wind, blue sails straining, heeled till the edge of the decking touched water. A single figure sat in the stern, hands upon the tiller, staring straight ahead.

There was a small garden shed leaning to against the wall of the kitchen. In it, apart from gardening tools and a small electric mower, was a useful-looking bicycle.

Tina decided to cycle down to the village.

She expected to see the village street packed with tourists, as it had been on their way through in the taxi; but there was not a soul in sight as she pedalled down in the direction of the tiny harbour in the quiet of the late afternoon. And yet – she was quite distinctly aware of being watched.

Glancing sidelong rather quickly, she caught the movement of a lace curtain slipping back into place. Looking up into an eyeless window, she was just in time to see a pale face slide away in suspect haste. Somewhere near at hand a dog barked – but was instantly silenced by what could only have been a brutal blow: the animal gave a yelp of pain and no more.

The shopping area comprised a fishmonger's whose window was placarded with whitewashed lettering announcing fresh mackerel, lobsters, crabs and mussels daily – but commencing at eight o'clock in the morning: the shop was empty and firmly marked 'closed'. Next to it stood a baker's, also closed. Opposite, an emporium announcing itself in stuck-on lettering as W. PENLEE - GENERAL STORES, TOBACCO-NIST, CONFECTIONER & NEWSPAPERS prompted Tina to go in.

'Yes?' Her questioner was a dour-looking, grey-faced man in a shapeless seaman's jersey and moleskin trousers. He stared at Tina short-sightedly through rimless glasses and waited patiently for her to make her wants known. To her delight, he did not appear to recognize her from the TV. And that was a relief.

She asked if he would deliver her papers, and he said that, yes, Clifftop Cottage came within his delivery round, and that would be twenty pence extra. What papers did she want? Tina gave him a list of dailies, Sunday papers, plus her favourite magazines. The only hitch appeared to be tomorrow – Sunday – when she would have to take pot luck with what happened to be around at such short notice. And what was her name? May – was that Mrs or Miss? Tina settled for Miss. She offered to pay a week in advance, but he seemed half offended by the idea, so she let it go at that, and left.

The harbour – or haven, for there was no more than one arm of a harbour wall that imperfectly enclosed the inlet and protected it from the south-west – was at low water, and a score of small fishing craft lay like beached dolphins, forlorn upon their sides. There was no one in sight save a solitary, blue-clad figure in seaboots and stocking cap, leaning against the harbour wall and staring out to sea with his back to Tina.

She remounted her bike and pedalled back up the main street, turning into the rutted path that the estate agents described as a private road. Going up was a lot more arduous than coming down.

A surprise awaited her when she let herself in through the solarium door, which, contrary to what she knew to be country ways, she had firmly locked upon leaving.

Someone had delivered a box inside the door.

It was the size of an old-fashioned grocer's biscuit box: the kind that used to be set out on corner-shop counters in her young days, the lids removed to display custard creams, fine arrowroot, chocolate wholemeal and the like. A single piece of thick string was knotted round the box, which bore no label, no name and address – though it had to be for her. But from whom? Strange.

She picked it up – found it to be quite heavy – and carried it through into the kitchen to open up.

Ever frugal, Tina carefully untied the string instead of

28

cutting through it, and raised the lid. The thing inside was wrapped in waxed paper.

As she lifted it out, she experienced a curious sense of *déjà vu* – thinking in the very same instant that she knew the reason why.

Nor was she wrong. . . .

Its weight, the shape of it, the feel of it – these all provided her memory with the key. Even before the thing was unwrapped and lying there on the kitchen work top with its dead eyes staring sightlessly up at her, she had known it was a – to her – familiar object: a portion of the human anatomy with which, in her calling, she was intimately familiar.

But though a seasoned – not to say case-hardened – forensic pathologist, Tina May was also a human being; a woman, moreover, gentle and tender-hearted in the bargain. Furthermore, in her very nervous and susceptible state, she had been given a bad scare.

And so she screamed at the sight of the severed head that lay before her – just like anyone would have.

The shock having passed, the trauma dispersed, Tina was able to do what any but one of her calling would have found quite impossible: to examine the specimen before her with a quiet professional detachment and mild scientific interest – as if it had been lying on a slab in a dissecting room.

The subject was male. Aged between forty-five and fifty. Well nourished, clear skin. Teeth – she opened the mouth (having put on rubber gloves) – mostly all there, and plenty of expensive dental work: gold fillings in the front, an elaborate splint across four, five and six upper right, and recent scaling. Slightly receding brown hair turning grey, but touched up with one of those progressive dyes that men use. Eyes – they stared straight at her – dark brown and myopic-looking. The slight indentation of a spectacle frame over the bridge of the nose confirmed the latter.

The head had been severed – she turned it over on its side –

after death. And by a skilled hand using a sharp knife, and a saw to cut between the third and fourth cervical vertebrae.

Time of death: impossible to say. The head had been refrigerated. And by its feel, had not long been exposed to the outside air again. But it had been chilled while still fresh.

The man had died – been murdered? – and the head neatly sliced off, then put into a refrigerator or deep freeze. And taken out – she removed a glove and laid her hand against a chill cheek – within the last few hours.

But why had it arrived here? And how – with the door locked?

They were questions that lay outside her competence to answer: why anyone would contrive the means to deliver the severed head of a complete stranger into her possession was beyond all belief.

Fortunately, it did not lie within her province to have to find the answer. . . .

Dermot Heymans' list of 'useful local people' included that of the village policeman. Tina rang the number, but no one answered the call. The address was given as The Police House, Back Street. Carefully replacing the head in the box, tying it up with the string, and laying the thing down where she had found it, she got onto the bicycle and pedalled down to seek out the lawman.

She found the police house in Back Street by questioning a trio of urchins who were playing marbles in the gutter outside the general store. It proved to be a neat modern villa with its styling lettered on a blue lamp over the door.

Tina knocked, but received no reply.

'He'll be back home for his tea at six sharp – he always gets back at six sharp.' The speaker was a pinched-faced woman of indeterminate age, who called to Tina over the party fence from the next-door front garden. She wore a scarf round her head to hide a complete set of curlers.

'Thank you,' said Tina. 'It's nearly six, so I'll wait.'

30

'I do his meals for him, by arrangement,' said the woman. 'He's not married, you see. Not any longer. Not properly.'

'Oh, yes?' responded Tina.

'Well, here comes Albert now,' said the other, as a sturdy figure in uniform blue dismounted from a cycle at the gate and came forward with an interrogative look at the stranger by his front door. 'Lady to see you, Albert,' said Tina's informant. 'Didn't say what her business was,' she added.

'Doctor May, isn't it?' he responded. 'Heard you was staying at Clifftop. Anything I can do for you, like?'

Tina glanced sidelong at his neighbour, who was all ears and eyes.

'Could I – um – have a word with you, officer?' she asked.

He took her point. 'I'll be round to fetch my meal shortly, Mrs Slyte,' he said. 'Just pop it in the oven and I'll be with you in a tick.'

'No need,' she said huffily. 'It's cold. Come when you like.'

'This way, Doctor,' said the policeman, opening the door. ' 'Fraid the place is in a bit of a mess, but my missus, she's left me and gone back to her mother. What was it you wanted to see me about?'

They stood together in the small hall, face to face. He was thick-set and athletic-looking, like a rugby player. For all that he was what Tina had come to categorize as 'all copper', with a copper's air of appraising one, waiting to determine if one was 'one of Us, or one of Them'; all her police friends at Scotland Yard and elsewhere were the same.

'I've had a visitor,' she began. 'Whoever it was has been and gone and left no message – only something's been left behind.'

He had a broken nose, with a pair of very washed-out blue eyes set closely to it; the eyes narrowed.

'Something left behind,' he repeated. 'Like – what?'

Tina took a deep breath. 'Frankly, I'd rather you came and saw it for yourself,' she said, 'because, quite honestly, I don't think you'd believe me if I told you what it is. You'd think – oh, I don't know – you'd think I'd been drinking, or something.'

He grinned to show a mouthful of very white teeth, whose perfection was marred only by two false top incisors.

'All right, Doctor,' he responded. 'I'll buy it. Let's go.'

They cycled, side by side, down Back Street, watched by Mrs Slyte through a gap in her lace curtains. Police Constable Tuttle – as he had introduced himself along the way – dismounted and pushed his cycle up the steep path to the cottage, and Tina did likewise.

'What time was it that your visitor came?' he asked. And she told him the approximate times between which she had been out.

'Did you leave the place locked?' Tina told him, and he showed approval of the fact that she had not followed the country custom.

Leaving their cycles leaning up against the wall, they went to the front door, which Tina opened with her latchkey. In the moment of so doing, she had a premonition as hard and certain as the feel of a knife in the hand.

'He's been back again – my visitor!' she breathed.

'How do you know?' asked Tuttle.

Tina made no reply; she went in, the constable following on her heels. The door into the passage was open, and she could see that the kitchen door – which she remembered closing – was ajar.

They entered the solarium in that order, she leading. One glance towards the outer door was enough to tell her that her premonition was not only correct, but that the unknown visitor had come back for a reason:

'It's gone – he's taken it away again!' she said dully.

'Well, then you might as well tell me what it was, now,' he replied with commendable patience.

And so – she did just that.

He was very patient with her: sat down at the kitchen table when he saw it was going to be a long job, took out his notebook and pencil and laboriously wrote down her statement, repeating her every word before committing it to paper. Then he went through the whole thing again.

'It was a head, you say? A man's head, and it felt like it had come out of a fridge?'

'Yes.' She felt her voice getting shrill; they had already been over that part.

'And you've never seen him before in your life – the chap whose head it was?'

She felt her nerve ends knotting up inside her.

'I've already said so!' she cried. '*Three* times!'

He nodded; closed his notebook and put his pencil back into the top pocket of his tunic. 'Well, I won't question you further, Doctor,' he said. 'I'll call in tomorrow morning, when maybe you'll have given the matter some thought and be able to add to your statement with a bit more detail, like.'

'But – aren't you going to do anything – *now?*' she cried.

He looked surprised. 'Of course, ma'am,' he replied. 'I shall phone this information through to HQ, and they'll do what they see fit.' He rose and picked up his helmet. 'And I'll be back to see you in the morning. At about – say – half eleven.'

'He doesn't believe me – he doesn't believe me! He thinks I'm imagining things!'

It had to be faced. A severed head on a Saturday afternoon in a remote Cornish fishing village took a bit of swallowing. One hoped, however, that Tuttle's superiors would take a more serious view of her claim.

Meanwhile, there was nothing she could do. Best to put the whole thing out of her mind. . . .

It had been a long day, and she was hungry. The well-stocked fridge yielded the makings of a plain omelette, cheese and biscuits and half a bottle of Muscadet. She had a shower after supper, locked and bolted all the doors carefully and went to bed with *A Tale of Two Cities* till she became heavy-eyed enough to turn out the light.

33

She was uneasily drifting off when she heard a tiny skittering in the rafters above her head, and called to mind the old countryman's saying that if you hear nothing it's a mouse, but if you hear a mouse it's a rat; she was contemplating the wisdom of this when sleep overtook her.

Though she slept soundly, the dream came to her very forcibly, and once she woke up screaming and sticky with sweat.

The clamour of church bells woke her at ten-thirty – or it may have been the sound of a motor scooter in the lane. She got up and took a cold shower, put on a kettle for coffee and went to see if the scooter rider had brought her Sunday paper. He had – and also, with great thoughtfulness, a bottle of milk and a loaf of bread.

Still in her dressing gown she breakfasted off toast and coffee in the solarium; and the sea was a sheet of beaten blue glass speckled with diamonds of sunlight over which the gulls soared, swooped and screamed lustily.

The best that W. Penlee had to offer in the way of journalistic fare was the *Sunday Courier*, which was far and away from being Tina's favourite Sabbath newspaper, being largely concerned with the seamier side of life, lightly spiced with pictures of cuddly animals and the doings of the Royal Family. It had also, on two occasions that she could name, personally attacked her and had also coined the sobriquet 'corpse doctor'.

She turned over the pages and sampled the limp, unappetizing fare:

'I WAS POP-IDOL'S MOLL . . .'

POST OFFICE LOVE-NEST WINS WIFE DECREE . . .

HAS ZACH COLENSO GOT AIDS? . . .

SEX-CHANGE PRIEST CLAIMS DAMAGES . . .

And a lot more.

It was then, just as she was about to throw the paper aside, that another headline stayed her hand:

There was a scarcely recognizable photo of her in dark glasses, coming out of the TV studio.

The piece underneath, written by the paper's 'ace' reporter, Monica Vane, with whom Tina had crossed swords on a previous occasion, was a subtle mixture of half-truths, idle speculation and downright lies, yet so cunningly contrived that even a person in the know would scarcely have been able to discern the joins holding the thing together:

Glamorous Tina May (B.SC., M.D., Hanley-Parker Gold Medallist in Bacteriology, Grenville Prizeman, Sutton Scholar, and Van Dyke Waterlow Student – according to *Who's Who in Medicine & Surgery*), star of the long-running TV hit *The Pathologist*, is reported to be suffering from a severe nervous breakdown. Trouble began during the recording of a show for the forthcoming autumn series, when the beautiful Corpse Doctor repeatedly fluffed her lines, burst into tears, then flew off the handle at her producer Simon Elles, calling him names when he quite gently ticked her off.

'POSTURING POOVE' DENIAL

Elles was not available for comment when our reporter rang him, but his secretary categorically stated that there is no truth in the rumour that Dr May referred to her producer as ' a bloody posturing poove'. Nevertheless, all's not well at TV House, and what is certain is that only two of the autumn shows have been recorded and that Tina has been 'relieved of duties' on full pay (estimated at £120,000 a year plus £20,000 per show).

PSYCHIATRIC TREATMENT

The plot thickens with the news that Tina has been receiving psychiatric treatment from Society Shrink Dr Dermot (Funny Guy) Heymans, Harley Street medic-about-town. She and Heymans dined together last week at Heymans' favourite nosherie and the fair pathologist was seen to be in tears. The upshot of it all is that Tina has departed to stay at Heymans' luxury villa 'somewhere in Cornwall' at a rental of £950 a week to – in the reported words of her resident secretary Maggie Wainwright – 'have her nervous breakdown in peace'.

Tina had scarcely finished reading this scurrilous rubbish when the phone rang. It was – almost predictably – Maggie, and she was in tears.

'What can you be thinking of me, Tina?' she sobbed. 'I never said any such *thing*. . . .'

'Of course you didn't, dear,' said Tina, placating her.

'Those people rang me after you'd left and asked if it was true you'd gone to Cornwall,' said Maggie. 'Since they didn't even seem to know the name of the village, I didn't see any harm in just admitting that you had. And that's all they asked me.

'That was it. Nothing else was said. They just rang off.

'You do believe me, don't you, Tina?'

'Of course I do, Maggie. Look, I've come across these people before, Monica Vane included. Truth with them is strictly something to kick around and bend into shape just where they want it to fit.

'Forget it, Maggie – I shall. Now – any further news of interest?'

'Only that young detective rang up again. . . .'

'Detective Sergeant Vance – what had he got to say?'

'I've written it down here. He said that he's inquired into the Stewart death and you'll be interested to hear that she and Holmes entered into a mutual life insurance arrangement whereby the pair of them, as common-law man and wife, were covered for forty thousand pounds, the survivor being the beneficiary. It appears that Holmes has already lodged his claim, but that the insurance company is jibbing at the pay-out.'

'Well, well – the plot thickens.'

'What was that you said, Tina?'

'Nothing. Is that all, then?'

'Yes. How are you getting on? Did you remember to get some provisions in?'

'No – but there's enough in the fridge and freezer to feed a

36

regiment for six months, and some kind soul remembered to provide me with fresh bread and milk this morning. And I've got a bicycle. I'm in clover.'

With a brief exchange of good wishes they rang off – and Tina decided to go out for a walk and try to begin to sort things out in her mind.

Quite close by the end of the cottage garden there was a steep and very rickety-looking wooden staircase leading down the sheer cliff face to the beach far below. 'One minute from the beach' – so the estate agent's brochure had said: provided one jumped, thought Tina wryly.

She had seen storm clouds massing above the horizon to the south, blotting out the sun and casting long shadows across the white sand, so she had dressed herself for every eventuality in a mackintosh over her shirt and jeans, with a headscarf tied under her chin. And she carried a stout walking stick for company.

The wooden steps were more substantial underfoot than they appeared. She was down in a little over a minute, and a few drops of rain touched her cheek as she trod the white, yielding sand.

There was not a soul in sight. To her left, the beach ended in a tumbled mass of black granite boulders that had been placed there as a bastion of defence against the sea, protecting the harbour wall. To the right – westwards – the coastline stretched in a splendid curve to the next headland about two miles distant as the crow flies: she decided to walk in that direction.

Closer to the shoreline, where the waves lapped and spent themselves in many-coloured foam and dribbled away to nothing, the sand was more firmly packed and the going easier. From there, also, she had a better view of the clifftop high above. West of the dark roof and upper windows of the cottage, the shining windows of the solarium, and the nodding lupins' heads that marked the limit of the garden, a

37

scrubland of gorse and stunted pines took over – stretching as far as the eye could see along the curve of the bay. A whole army could have lain in hiding up there, watching everything that moved along the shoreline. Quite suddenly, from feeling utterly alone and unmolested, Tina sensed that she was being watched – just as she had felt it in the seemingly deserted village the previous afternoon.

Surely that was a face which moved quickly out of sight up there when she turned. And wasn't it the sudden flash of a woman's skirt which had snaked round behind that gorse bush? She quickened her pace – automatically – as if to put the watcher, or watchers, real or imagined, further behind her.

A little further on – and the cottage roof had now slipped out of her sight – she turned and looked again. There was no suspicion of a face this time, no flash of colour; but, surely, the branch of a pine tree had stirred most unaccountably – almost as if someone – something – had brushed past it. . . .

She told herself not to be so silly. There might well be children up there, playing peek-a-boo with her, as children will. No harm in that. Shrugging off the irrational unease, she stepped it out even more quickly – towards a finger of rock which, descending in a steep slope from the clifftop, ended close by the shoreline, forming the limit of a small bay within the larger bay.

She did not look round again till she was within a dozen paces of the granite mass with its attendant boulders and rock pools. This time she established – quite firmly and to her complete satisfaction – that there was no one watching her from the clifftop.

'Ah, good morning to you. Trying hard to rain, don't you think?'

The sound of the voice made her start: it was so close, and oddly challenging. Turning, she saw a tall, willowy figure all in black coming from behind the finger of rock. Rusty black from head to foot: an old-fashioned, tall-crowned hat; a cassock, shiny at the elbows from long wear; a furled umbrella

38

in one bony hand – everything black, save for a clerical collar around the man's scrawny neck. A parson – a man of God, walking the beach on that Sabbath morning.

'Hello,' said Tina, unabashed, now that her initial surprise was over. 'Yes, I felt a few spots just now.'

He was quite elderly: she put him at around seventy-odd; and there was a certain cyanosis around his mouth and a thickening of the wrist and finger joints that spoke of arthritis; but the eyes that fixed her from behind rimless pebble glasses were shrewd and piercing, though rheumy.

'I think I am addressing the famous Doctor May,' he said.

'That's so,' admitted Tina. And she supposed that a man of the cloth would not be asking for her autograph. 'I'm Tina May.'

'Didn't see you in church this morning,' he said, with a twinkle of eye that denied any hint of a reproof.

'I'm not a churchgoer,' admitted Tina, adding: 'I suppose you would call me an agnostic, er. . . .'

'Wakeley,' he supplied, 'Arthur Wakeley, vicar of St Botolph's, Trepoll Haven. Your religious convictions apart, Doctor, the church is of considerable architectural merit, if you are interested in architecture. A fine Early English nave, Perpendicular apse and east door. The pews and most of the wooden furnishings are, I'm afraid, late Victorian. I read about you in the newspaper this morning.'

'Really?' replied Tina, surprised.

The shrewd eyes softened. 'I should like you to think,' he said, 'that, though you are not one of my flock and, indeed, what you are pleased to call an agnostic, you would not hesitate to call upon my assistance if your troubles get too much for you.'

'That's – very kind of you, Mr Wakeley,' responded Tina with some embarrassment.

'The pressures of modern life,' said Wakeley, 'bear down upon us all. You would scarcely believe that, even in this peaceful corner of the land' – he gestured about him to cliffs, harbour, headland – 'the rigours of today's living are enough

39

to drive even the simple-hearted and unworldly to a state of despair. How much more so must you, Doctor May, with the many burdens that you bear, be afflicted?

'As I have read, this morning, in the press.'

'One shouldn't believe everything one reads in the newspapers, Mr Wakeley,' said Tina. 'Particularly *some* newspapers.'

'So I have always believed,' replied the other. He paused for a moment to look at a seagull that, flying overhead, suddenly espied them and bated away as if in alarm. 'But, nevertheless, where there is smoke, there is invariably fire.'

'Well, I assure you that the report upon my condition in today's *Courier* is much exaggerated,' said Tina. 'Believe me.'

The shrewd eyes searched her out from head to foot. 'I am inclined to accept what you say, Doctor,' he replied. 'But – nevertheless. . . .'

'Yes, Mr Wakeley?'

'Nevertheless, please remember that my door is always open to those who suffer, or are in doubt, or want, or – *fear*. Please remember that.'

'I will,' said Tina. 'And thank you.'

'Would you care to join me in a brief prayer – here and now?'

'Not now,' she replied. 'But thank you for the thought.'

He smiled: it was a tired, joyless smile. 'Then I will bid you good day, Doctor,' he said, and, turning, walked away from her towards the cliff from which he had appeared. It was then she saw that the far side of the finger of rock was in fact one wall of a gully or cleft in the rocky bastion that fronted the sea, and that there was an inclined path through the cleft that must surely lead back to the village.

One day she must explore the path; but not now, not in the company of the rather disconcerting vicar with the surprising taste in Sabbath reading. Maybe, she reasoned, the Reverend Mr Wakeley took a scurrilous rag like the *Courier* because it fed his morbid interest in the wayward members of his own calling whose doings provided one of the classic ingredients of that journal. And because of that, he had learned all about her supposed nervous breakdown, together with all the spicy details cooked up in the tortuous mind of Monica Vane.

Was it only because of that that he had showed so much concern for her well-being, or was there something else? She rather thought there might have been. Something in his expression had worried her. And his concern – call it solicitude – had been out of all proportion to her need. Was not the solicitude something that was directed towards himself? That was certainly how it had come across to her.

She tried the 'Synonym Game', a mental exercise that had been very popular in her Upper Sixth form English language group at school.

Solicitude equals, say, disquiet.

Disquiet – call it dread.

Dread is a synonym for fear.

And that begged the question: just what was the Reverend Mr Wakeley afraid of?

Three

Time was getting on. Her need to return by eleven-thirty and the arrival of PC Tuttle was underscored by a lightning flash from the tumbled clouds, a crash of thunder and a sudden downpour of rain; she turned about, hugged the collar of her mack closely about her ears and set off back at a swift pace.

She arrived at the foot of the staircase just as the rain ceased and the great arc of a rainbow displayed itself right across the bay from headland to headland. She stood at the top of the steps and wondered at the majesty of its beauty for some time before she turned to go into the cottage.

PC Tuttle was standing in the shelter of the solarium porch.

His attitude was quite different from what it had been the previous evening. Then, he had shown a tolerant indulgence, the sort of irritating masculine reaction to a supposedly hysterical female who thinks she has 'seen' something. Today, it was something harder, harsher, more ingrained. She was soon to find out why.

He began by taking her right through her statement again as if they had never touched upon the subject before: he quibbled at every point, every detail, doubling back on the questions time and time again, as if by getting a slight variation in her answers he might trap her into a lie.

Finally, she could stand it no longer. She faced him squarely.

'Officer, it seems to me that we're wasting each other's time,' she said.

Tuttle laid down his pencil and regarded her quizzically.

'Let's get this straight, Doctor,' he said. 'You say someone left a head with you. Now, in your particular line of work, I suppose severed heads are pretty commonplace. With me, they're not. I've been in the Force for fourteen years, coming on fifteen, and I've never come across a severed head in all that time – 'spite of traffic accidents, dead bodies washed up on the foreshore and the like. To me, your story takes a lot of swallowing. Like it would with most folks.'

Tina stared at him, wide-eyed. 'You really *don't* believe me, do you?' she snapped.

'It isn't that, Doctor. It's. . . .' He searched for the words to express his meaning.

'You think I'm lying. That I made it up. But, for heaven's sake, man, why in God's name would I make up such a thing as that?' cried Tina.

He avoided her gaze; becoming suddenly interested in the point of his pencil.

'Well, Doctor,' he began. 'Since you ask me straight out, like. . . .'

Tina gasped, unbelieving – yet knowing the truth of it. . . .

'You think I'm out of my mind!' she cried. 'You read that rubbish in your grubby newspaper this morning, and you think you've got me taped. Not as a professional woman – a person of some substance: educated, expert, perhaps even rather eminent.

'Oh, no – not you! You don't see me like that – as I am. To you, I'm just another silly, hysterical woman who's indulging herself in a nervous breakdown!

'That's how you see me – you damned, narrow-minded, pig-headed – *man*!'

And then, realizing the enormity of her insult: 'Oh, officer, that was quite unforgivable of me! I *am* sorry – *truly* sorry!'

By fervent protestation and total withdrawal of her remarks, Tina went some way to mending her fences with PC Tuttle, but it was quite obvious that her outburst had only served to confirm his belief that she was unbalanced. Nevertheless, he wrote up his supplementary report and got her to read it through and initial it to that effect. He then took his leave, promising to inform her of any reaction from his headquarters.

Tina watched him go off down the lane, certain in the knowledge that he would share his experience with his neighbour Mrs Slyte – in the strictest confidence, of course – over his 'dinner'.

Overwrought and on edge, she was in no condition to fancy anything to eat; instead, she poured herself a stiff whisky and, slumping down in a sitting-room armchair, tried to come to terms with the appalling event which had turned her 'retreat' into a ready-made nightmare.

The question was: *who* had put the head inside the cottage?

Think, girl – think! A process of ratiocination. . . .

What manner of person – man or woman – had left the head and (presuming that it was the same person) had then taken it away again?

First: whoever had put the head inside the cottage must be in possession of a key.

Second: it follows that this person is familiar with the cottage.

But, supposing that he – or she – didn't know enough about the cottage to be aware that a new visitor had taken possession? Yes, that made sense, and would account for the head being left (a hiding place?).

But having left the head in the cottage, the intruder then saw her – Tina – coming back from the shop, didn't have time to run back into the cottage and snatch up the head, but simply bolted in panic down the staircase to the beach.

That made sense – a sort of sense.

And the conclusion: from that, the mysterious someone has been accustomed to the run of the cottage and, by inference, knows and is known to Dermot Heymans – but is not in close enough contact with the owner of Clifftop to have been informed by him that Tina May was taking up residence.

So. . . .

Tina poured herself another drink and, with her premises and conclusion in mind, reconstructed a scene in her imagination:

The mystery person, having deposited the head inside the outer door of the solarium and relocked it, pauses for a moment in the garden upon hearing footsteps coming up the lane from the village. At any moment the newcomer will appear. What to do? No time to unlock the door and recover the head. There is only one course open – flight.

Moments later, perhaps, turning to look back in headlong retreat down the staircase to the beach, the mysterious person sees Tina May pushing her cycle up the path towards the cottage. Who, he asks himself (or, she asks herself) is this woman?

And what next?

Next, Tina pictured herself cycling down the drive on her way to fetch the village policeman. The mysterious intruder, lingering on the staircase, sees Tina May and grabs at the opportunity to go back up to the cottage and recover the head. And escapes by way of the beach staircase before she and the constable return.

Very satisfactory solution. *Quod erat demonstrandum.*

I wonder? thought Tina.

The alternative was not so attractive: this was to suppose that there were two persons involved with the severed head: the first one having left it in the cottage for the second to pick up.

Clumsy. Illogical. But, worst of all, it was a hypothesis that stood or fell upon her – Tina's – comings and goings. To make the hypothesis work, she just *had* to have gone for a walk when person one, not knowing that she was staying at Clifftop, left the head at the cottage; and that number two chanced to pick the short time – a quarter of an hour or so – when she was fetching PC Tuttle, to make the collection. No – down with the two-person theory: too many coincidences.

There was one other consideration: when she returned to

45

the cottage with the policeman and had the premonition that the strange visitor had come back again: was that merely a case of *déjà vu*, or had she seen or heard something – subconsciously, subliminally? – that sparked off the notion in her mind? It was worth thinking about.

Tina was doing just that when there came a knock on the front door.

'Hello, you don't know me, even though I'm in the happy position – like so many others – of knowing you, if only through the media. I'm Glenda Wakeley.'

The visitor was tall, blonde, and beautifully turned-out in a casual tweed two-piece, a Hermès scarf draped casually over her shoulders. Blue eyes shaded to green. Impeccably made-up. Aged anything from thirty-odd to forty-plus, and the possessor of the kind of beauty sometimes described as 'evergreen'.

Tina took her proffered hand. 'Do come in,' she said. 'Wakeley? Then you must be . . .'

'Arthur Wakeley's wife,' said the other, rather quickly, thereby – and to Tina's surprise and instant relief – ridding her of the quite understandable assumption that the blonde beauty must be the old vicar's daughter. 'Actually, we're "Honourables",' she continued, 'Arthur being the young brother of a bloody lord, would you believe?' She looked all about her: vibrant, enthusiastic. 'You know, I simply love this cottage. I came here often when Ellis Duke was alive. Did you know Ellis, Doctor May?'

Tina shook her head. 'No – was he by chance? . . .'

'The artist. He painted the murals' – Glenda Wakeley pointed down the room to the hideous figure obtruding through the end wall – 'Isn't that stunning? Terrifying – yes. But quite, quite stunning.' Her beautiful mask registered concern. 'Don't you like it, then? Does it, perhaps, upset you?'

'It's not the sort of thing I'd choose to live with in my own home,' admitted Tina. 'My taste runs to something more –

46

relaxing.' And then, remembering civility, she added: 'Would you like some coffee?'

The other's blue-green eyes swept meaningfully towards the drinks table and Tina's half-empty glass. 'If you're imbibing, I'd much rather join you in something a trifle more vivid,' she said with a touch of mischief.

They both laughed.

Face to face in the easy chairs before the fireplace, glasses in hands, there quickly sparked between them a certain atmosphere of – call it mateyness. Relaxed, friendly, Glenda Wakeley crossed her legs, offered Tina a cigarette, asked if she minded, lit herself one, puffed out a smoke ring, watched it float up to the ceiling, smiled across at her companion and said: 'You married, or anything, Tina? You don't mind if I call you Tina? I feel as if I've known you for ages – like most of your fans, I suppose.'

'No, I'm not married, Glenda,' replied Tina. 'I once was, but we broke up. The dream faded with the realities. I've never tried it again. All the nice people were either married already, or weren't interested in me, or' – she thought of Johnny Kettle, her mentor, father-figure, her everything, now gone for ever – 'or thought they were too old for me.'

When she had said the words, she realized that she had all inadvertently put her foot in it, and felt the colour mount in her cheeks. She glanced across at her companion. She need not have worried: Glenda Wakeley was chuckling with amusement.

'They're never too old for one,' said the other cheerfully. 'As a husband, I mean. Let's face it, dear – what's a husband? Someone to sit opposite one over the breakfast table after the honeymoon night, and upon whom one speculates: "So this is the character with whom I have got to perform this charade, day in and day out, night in and night out, for the rest of our natural lives".

'What could be more boring? And what does it matter if the man's ten – twenty – thirty years older than one? With a younger man there's always an initial excitement, but

47

let a little time go by and they're all the same. Boring.

'But meanwhile' – her eyes twinkled – 'there's always another man – maybe young, maybe old – *but most of all new* – waiting in the wings.' She laughed out loud. 'Do you find me outrageous?' she asked.

'Yes,' admitted Tina, and laughed with her.

Without being asked, the surprising blonde went over to the drinks table and refilled her glass; Tina declined another.

'Tell me more about Ellis Duke,' said Tina, the combination of two drinks and her ebullient companion having greatly mitigated the effects of the last twenty-four hours' disturbing events. 'I was told that he killed himself.'

'That he did, poor darling,' confirmed the other. 'He committed suicide out of love for me.' She lit herself another cigarette, and Tina noticed that her hands were trembling slightly.

'I see,' murmured Tina.

'Not quite, you don't, dear,' replied her companion. 'But you will, you will.' She sat back in her chair. 'Ellis was brilliant, but flawed. And he was mad – quite mad. You must know that, Tina. Surely your friend Doctor Heymans told you. Heymans was treating Ellis right up to the time he died. Rented him this cottage for over a year and Ellis repaid him in part by painting the murals.'

'Yes, I know all that,' admitted Tina.

Glenda Wakeley took a long pull at her drink, and continued: 'Ellis was into the occult. That much shows from his murals, of course. He was a great proselytizer: held seances and things here in the cottage and gathered about him a lot of – I suppose you'd call them disciples.

'My husband didn't approve.'

Tina thought back to the austere figure in rusty black whom she had encountered on the beach that morning. The very notion that the bland and unrepentant hedonist before her was his wife was unlikely enough; that he would also look kindly upon occult goings-on of the sort suggested by the murals in Clifftop Cottage was asking too much.

'However,' went on her companion, 'Arthur or no Arthur, Ellis continued with his seances and his circle of disciples remained with him – myself included, though to tell you the truth I wasn't hooked on the mystique so much as on the man. There was something very elemental about Ellis. It showed in his work, of course, and also in his life style. The life style became a little depressed, however, when he finally got through the last of a legacy he'd been living on for most of his adult life, and had to rely upon the proceeds of his art.

'As you can imagine, my dear, with his kind of subject matter – which was all he produced – he didn't prosper a lot. In fact, by the time of his death, he owed money everywhere: picture framers and colour merchants, groceries, wine merchants, maintenance for his two ex-wives, the tax man – most of all the tax man. And he was also into drugs – which finally finished him off when he didn't have the money to keep himself supplied.

'It all ended when he asked me to run away with him. He had this crazy idea of going to the States and starting again. His agent had fixed an exhibition of his work in New York and it had caught the public fancy the way things will – just a flash in the pan. He said there was fame and a million waiting for him over there and would I go with him.' She laughed throatily and stubbed out her cigarette.

'You refused?' asked Tina.

'By this time, he was beginning to be rather boring,' replied Glenda Wakeley. 'So I told him there was nothing doing.' She lit another cigarette. 'The night after, he went down on to the beach and walked out to sea. And kept walking. . . .'

In the long silence that followed, the brass travelling clock on the oak chimneypiece tinkled the hour of five.

'Great Scott!' exclaimed Glenda Wakeley, leaping up. 'Is it that late? My dear, if we're to be friends – and I hope we're to be friends while you're here – you must learn to harden your heart and stop me from babbling on.

'I must go.' She reached out and took Tina's hand, and the blue-green eyes were searching. 'For a person having a

49

nervous breakdown, you strike me as being uncommonly level-headed,' she said. 'Or was it – as you implied to my old man when you met him this morning – mostly newspaper talk?'

'Almost entirely newspaper talk,' replied Tina.

The other nodded. 'I thought so. No – don't get up. I'll see myself out. Thanks for the drinks.'

She passed at the door and looked back – particularly towards the mural on the far wall. 'Ellis grew to be a tremendous bore,' she said, 'but there's no doubt about it – this place has never been the same since he left.'

Tina sat quietly for a while after her visitor had left, turning over in her mind the content of the other's monologue, which she had found compulsively entertaining. The outgoing Mrs Wakeley, she decided, would be just about the last person in Trepoll Haven in whom to confide the account of the severed head, for it would be common gossip in the village before the day was out (if PC Tuttle, through his nosey next-door neighbour, hadn't begun the process already). A curiously fascinating woman, nevertheless and, yes, compulsively entertaining.

But – where had she set eyes on that Junoesque blonde beauty before?

She realized it in almost the next instant; was on her feet and racing across the room to the study, where she pulled aside the bookcase and revealed the painting of the human sacrifice.

Under the upraised knife, the victim lay as before, staring up at the dreadful creature who menaced her, a scream frozen upon her painted lips.

The face, the blue-green eyes, the blonde hair – and, presumably, the secrets of the undraped figure – were those of the wife of the vicar of St Botolph's, Trepoll Haven.

*

50

After a makeshift meal eaten without enthusiasm, she had an urge to phone Dermot Heymans, but without any very clear idea of how she was going to tackle him. One thing she was quite sure about: there was to be no mention of the head. Not yet. Not till she had quite recovered from the unpleasant experience of having been categorized by the village policeman as a hysterical neurotic. That had been bad enough in all conscience: the added prospect of Heymans dissecting her mind over the telephone and coming to the conclusion that she was hallucinating badly and was in need of constant supervision would be more than she could bear for one day.

But she needed to know a couple of things. . . .

Heymans answered her immediately – it was as if he might have been standing with his hand on the receiver:

'Tina, my dear. Lovely to hear your voice. How are you, and how's Clifftop?'

'Fine, just fine.'

'My dear, I have to tell you – there's been a most scandalous piece about you in the *Sunday Courier*. I don't take the rag, of course, but my housekeeper drew my attention. . . .'

'It's all right, Dermot. I saw it. It didn't upset me unduly. Just made me wild with anger, that's all.'

He laughed. 'A very healthy reaction, psychologically. How are you making out down there? Met anyone?'

'The vicar and his lady.'

'An ill-assorted couple – as you will have decided already. Glenda was the late Ellis Duke's girlfriend for a while. When she gets to know you better, she'll tell you that he killed himself for love of her.'

'She's told me already.'

'Has she now? Well, I doubt that Duke killed himself for unrequited love – his psychosis would never have moved him in that particular direction. On the other hand, Glenda would certainly never leave old Arthur Wakeley – not for Duke or for anyone else.'

'Why not – particularly?'

51

'Because Arthur, for all that he simply *has* to be thirty years older than she, is right out of the top drawer socially. An aristocrat. An Honourable, and his brother's a lord. It's as simple as that.'

Tina digested this piece of information, and said: 'I never would have guessed that of her. She struck me as being very basic – earthy, even. Not the social climber at all.'

'Glenda, my dear, is more subtle than you believe,' was Heymans' response to that.

'Oh, by the way, Dermot –' Tina met her reflection in the mirror above the telephone table and caught her expression in the act of adjusting itself to the task of asking the question which was the principal reason for calling Heymans. 'Do you happen to have a spare key of the cottage?'

'No, dear,' came the reply. 'I have one on my own key ring here. There was only one other – and you have it.'

'It's just that – I like to have a spare, in case I lose this one somewhere.'

'Of course. Well, you can always have one cut.'

'Do you suppose that Ellis Duke had a spare – or spares – cut?'

'I don't see why not. Why do you ask?'

'Oh, no reason,' replied Tina hastily. 'It's just that – I wondered if there might be one lying around in a drawer somewhere.'

'There might very well be.' He sounded uninterested. 'Well, my dear. Glad to hear you're settling in nicely. I may pop down and see you one weekend if I can get away. How will that be?'

'Oh, yes, that will be nice,' she said – rather too hastily. 'But not just yet, Dermot.'

'No, no, my dear. First, we must let the peace and quiet work its gentle wonders. Are you sleeping better already – or did you dream badly again last night?'

'No,' lied Tina.

'There – you see, Clifftop is beginning to exercise its magic balm already.'

'Yes,' she said. 'Well, I really must go, Dermot. Lovely to hear your voice. Thanks for everything. Oh' – she had a sudden thought – 'by the way, I may yet get around to taking you up on the suggestion of whitewashing over the murals.'

'You don't like them? Good for you.'

'I particularly don't like the one in the study.'

'Ah, the one depicting la belle Glenda in the process of being sacrificed by Ellis Duke in his role of the Devil.'

'Oh, it is supposed to be him – I had an idea it might be.'

'It was Duke, right enough. He had a regular witches' coven going down in Trepoll Haven right up till the time he died – and there's still vestiges of it around the place.'

'When was that, Dermot – when did he die?'

'Oh, about eight or nine months ago.'

'And he drowned himself?'

'That was presumed. He was seen wading out to sea in the moonlight. The body was never recovered, but that's normal on that stretch of the Cornish coast – they get swept out into the wastes of the Atlantic, you see.'

'Yes, I see.'

Another brief exchange of farewells, and she replaced the receiver, meeting her reflection in the mirror as she did so.

'Well,' she told herself aloud, 'at least we know that whoever brought the head wasn't given a key by Dermot. So it had to be Ellis Duke who handed it out, didn't it? So, my visitor knew Duke pretty well – a woman, without a doubt.

'A member of his coven?

'One wonders who were – or still are – the members of his coven. And did he, perhaps, give keys to all of them?

'I mustn't *ever* forget to lock and bolt all the doors at night!'

There was a portable radio in the cottage, but no TV. For this Tina was profoundly grateful, for she had decided to cut herself right off from the media – except for a glance at the newspaper headlines, to check that the world was still turning round. For the rest she had the collection of books she had brought with her, and they comprised old favourites, plus a few fairly formidable volumes that she had always promised herself to read when a suitable opportunity arose. There was, for instance, *War and Peace* – which she had calculatingly earmarked for if and when she had a protracted terminal illness. No need, now, to await that grim occasion: she would start it immediately after Sydney Carton had made his deathless sacrifice.

That night she took a cup of hot chocolate up to bed with her, along with a sleeping capsule and *Two Cities*. Of the bedrooms, she had chosen the larger of the two, which was over the study and bathroom and had windows on three sides: one overlooking the lane down to the village, another providing a distant picture-postcard view of the haven, and the one to the rear which gave out to a breathtaking panorama of beach, sea and sky. There was a most charming tester bed in this room, with fanciful silk hangings gathered back into pudgy fingers of little gilt cherubs attached to the uprights of the bed-head, and a feather mattress which was divinely comfortable. The rest of the furnishings were simple and austere: a dressing table of plain oak with a mirror set in an antique gilded picture frame, a Victorian button-back chair and chest of drawers, and a Georgian corner cupboard of the 'hanging' sort. She had been attracted to the latter as a possible place to store her modest library, but had found it to be locked.

Minutes later, showered, teeth cleaned, she sat sipping her hot chocolate, having taken the sleeper. The sun had gone down. There was no need to draw any curtains, for on her high promontory she was not overlooked on any side. The reading lamp cast long shadows across the room as she came to the end of a chapter and closed the book.

Before she had time to put out the light, her eyes closed and she drifted away into the preliminaries of a drugged sleep, only to be aroused by a gentle creaking, as if from a slowly-opening door. She bore it for a few moments, then tremulously opened her eyes.

54

What she saw brought a scream to her lips that was shocking even to herself, so that it became part of the dreadfulness. What she saw was the door of the corner cupboard fully opened – to disclose its gruesome content – staring out at her, goat's eyes wide and mouth agape – the head of the Devil from downstairs!

Four

Eyes closed in the pathetic belief that she could shut out the image, she continued to scream, but the vision still burned in her brain: the living, breathing, leering thing that looked out at her from inside the cupboard – the disembodied head lying upon a shelf.

Inevitably, her screams awakened her, and she sat up in bed, trembling, terribly afraid. She looked across at the corner cupboard. It was closed.

Determination triumphing over reluctance, she got out of bed and went across to the cupboard. It was, of course, still locked.

Running her eyes over the piece, she had an idea: what if the key had been put behind the moulding at the top of the cupboard? It was just the kind of place where one might half-hide it.

She reached up – and her fingers closed about – a key.

It fitted the lock and turned smoothly. All she had to do now was to open the door. . . .

Bracing herself, she did so. As she had expected – she a rational, intelligent and highly educated woman – the cupboard was empty of anything resembling a head, in fact it was completely empty.

With an involuntary shudder, she went back to bed and, for the first time since she was a little girl and sometimes scared of the dark, pulled the sheet over her face. Almost immediately, the drugged capsule took full effect and put her into a deep sleep.

*

That night, Tina relived again the full horror of the motorway pile-up in detail – an extension of the vision of the head which the capsule had revealed to her in its first manifestations. In this dream, the scene was sickeningly heightened by the presence of the Devil from downstairs. He dominated the tangled gallimaufry of blazing vehicles by looming above them all, one cloven hoof resting on the red-hot roof of the burning car containing the roasting man, hands extended towards her, taloned fingers beckoning her – Tina May – to come and join him in his hellish feast of death; and though she fought against a compulsion to obey, her very feet were dragged against her unconscious will, to be a part of the dreadful scene.

Tina was closing with the maw of flaming perdition when she was again woken by her own screams – and sat up in the bed, bathed in moonlight from the uncurtained windows.

When she had calmed herself, she got out of bed and, pouring a glass of water from a carafe on the side table, took it over to the south-facing window that looked out over cliff, sand and sea. Out across the moonlit, ruffled wavelets, the dark outlines of distant ships bore their white and coloured lights up and down the Channel, to the ports of the coast, and away to the west and the trackless Atlantic. It was a scene so peaceful that a warm balm was laid upon her troubled heart and she was able to creep back into her bed and trust herself to close her eyes again.

When she woke a cockerel was greeting the new day from one of the farms up on the heights beyond the village, and was answered by a dog barking down by the haven. She went down to the kitchen and put on a kettle for a cup of coffee. It had scarcely begun to sing towards a boil when the telephone rang in the living room.

It was PC Tuttle:

'Doctor May? Sorry to be calling you so early, but we've an officer – Detective Inspector Wainhouse – coming to see us from headquarters. That's to say, like, he's coming to interview you in connection with the alleged human

57

head that you claim to have come across on Saturday.

'Are you hearing me, Doctor?'

'Yes, I hear you, Officer!' she snapped. 'And I would point out that the head in question was not an "alleged" head, and that what you call my "claim" to having seen it was a statement of fact.'

'With respect, Doctor,' came the cold response, 'that will be for the inspector to decide. And I'd point out, ma'am, that Mr Wainhouse ain't a man to be trifled with – what's more, he's coming a long way to see you.'

'And what am I to infer from those observations?' demanded Tina.

'What I'm trying to say is, Doctor, that if having slept on it and thought things over in your mind, like, you wish to change your story about what you allege you saw yesterday, now would be the time to do it and save us all a lot of inconvenience. Not to mention the trouble you might be letting yourself in for.'

'I see,' replied Tina. 'Yes, I think I get your drift, Officer. Well, in reply, I have not changed my mind about what I saw yesterday – and I shall be looking forward to convincing your inspector on that score.'

'Very well, Doctor,' came the frigid reply. 'Expect the both of us to call upon you some time this morning.'

He rang off.

Tina, simmering with a repressed fury of righteous indignation, drank her coffee, toyed with some toast, and then showered and got dressed to receive her visitors. By that time the first of the morning's doubts had begun to overlay the bright self-confidence she had earlier known: after the manner of human frailty, her mind began to question if, indeed, she had imagined the whole ghastly episode of the severed head, and that the occurrence had been a phantasmagoria conjured up by her troubled subconscious. A disturbing extension of this kind of thinking was that everyone – not only PC Tuttle, and such as the *Sunday Courier* and their moronic readers, but also intelligent people like

Simon Elles and co. at the TV studios, together with top-flight alienist Dermot Heymans – believed her to be unbalanced.

She was well into this kind of negative and perniciously destructive thinking when the phone rang again. This time it was someone named Hargreaves, who described himself as the proprietor and resident manager of the North Park Holiday Camp – a conglomerate of caravans and holiday chalets that she had noticed when coming into Trepoll in the taxi.

'Doctor May, is it? Doctor, I'm sorry to trouble you, but we've had a tragic accident. Yes – a lady's come to grief in the swimming pool. Drowned? Well, we're trying hard at the moment to revive her, but I think it's touch and go. I tried our Doctor Strang, but he's out on his rounds.

'Yes, would you, please?

'Shall I send a car round for you, or? . . .

'You have a bike? Well, it's only a step.

'Yes, please. Oh, please hurry, Doctor!'

Tina did no more than snatch up her emergency bag, slip into a pair of sensible shoes for cycling, and set off down the lane. She could see the pantiled roofs of the chalets from Clifftop. From the village street it was all on the straight, and she was pedalling in through the brightly coloured gates of North Park Holiday Camp within minutes of receiving the call.

Hargreaves was a shortish, dumpy man in his early fifties. He came running. He was flustered, worried and apologetic. Fear of death, and awe at the presence of a TV celebrity, struggled for supremacy within him.

'Oh, I'm so grateful to you, Doctor. I heard from Mr Penlee that you were here, in fact it's all round the village that you're staying at Clifftop. This way, please. We put Mrs Wakeley in this empty chalet here. . . .'

'Did you say – Wakeley?' demanded Tina.

'The vicar's wife, yes,' replied Hargreaves. 'She comes in

for an early morning swim most days when it's fine. Early – so she can have the pool to herself. In here, Doctor – after you.'

The chalet was plainly furnished, with a bed that had been dragged out into the centre of the floor. Lying prone upon it, face turned sideways, was the Junoesque blonde of her previous day's acquaintance. She was wearing a plain white backless swimsuit and appeared to be unconscious – or dead. A muscular, athletic-looking man in his late twenties, early thirties, was squatting astride the still figure and performing the standard, approved life-saving and resuscitating procedure – and doing it very well. He did not pause, or even look up, when Tina felt the victim's pulses and raised the eyelids. But he threw her a savage glance when she sounded the upturned, bare back with her stethoscope.

'She's dead,' murmured Tina.

'Oh, my God!' breathed Hargreaves. And there came a chorus of horror from the people who were crowding at the open door and window.

The muscular young man paused for only a moment in his efforts and glared at Tina with close-set, button-black eyes.

'That's *what* you say – but it'll do no harm if I carry on in the hope – will it?' he snarled.

'No, it won't do any harm,' she replied, folding up her stethoscope.

'Lenny Jordan's our pool attendant,' whispered the camp proprietor in Tina's ear. 'He's got a gold medal for life-saving, so you can trust him to do his best, Doctor. It was he who found Mrs Wakeley lying in there, in the pool.'

'Lying, you say?' asked Tina. 'Submerged?'

'That's right. Up at the deep end. She must have bumped her head, or got cramp, or something. There was no one around to see it happen – it being so early in the morning.'

Lenny Jordan was still manfully working upon what Tina knew well to be a corpse. 'For how long has he been trying to revive her?' she murmured.

'Well, we lifted her out and he started trying to revive her on the side of the pool,' replied Hargreaves. 'Then we carried her in here and I went off to ring our doctor. After that, I phoned around to find you. Call it – oh – about half an hour ago when we got her out.' He stared anxiously at her. 'Is she – *quite* dead, Doctor?'

Tina nodded. 'But let him carry on – otherwise, he'll go through the rest of his life wondering if he missed snatching her back by a minute. From what you tell me, I'd guess she was probably gone when you lifted her out of the water.'

Presently, the muscular Jordan sat back on his hunkers and ceased his efforts. He remained for a while, chest heaving with sheer fatigue. Then he got down from the bed – with one reluctant glance back at the drowned woman.

'You'd better ring the police, Mr Hargreaves,' said Tina. 'Meanwhile, I'll make a preliminary examination of the body. Will you clear the room, please?'

There was a slight disturbance, a marked reluctance on the part of some of those present to be ejected from the death chalet and to be denied any further part as onlookers. The man Jordan, massive when standing upright in his T-shirt and brief white shorts, shook off Hargreaves' guiding arm as they went out through the door together, and he glared back at Tina. She looked away; heard him mutter something that included the words 'in the Sunday paper' and – though she was not sure – mouthed a phrase which sounded uncommonly like: 'Bleeding doctors – all the same'. But he was nearly beyond earshot, and she told herself she may have been mistaken.

Alone with the remains of Mrs Glenda Wakeley, Tina addressed herself to making the first – and very often most important – examination of a deceased subject.

She turned the corpse over on its back and carefully peeled off the still wet one-piece swimsuit. As she did so, she noticed something that caused her to pause and look again.

'That's odd,' she said aloud. 'Very odd – and I wouldn't have believed it of the smart woman I met yesterday.'

There was scarcely any loss of body temperature, and, of course, no onset of rigor mortis. The morning was already hot and she supposed that the pool was heated – so that made sense.

Marks on the body: there was an extensive bruise on the left temple, sustained before death – that could well have rendered her unconscious. (Slipped while running along the side, and hit her head on the edge as she fell? One of the commonest of pool accidents.)

There were other bruises – not strongly marked – on both wrists and on the left forearm. Tina was still puzzling over these factors when she turned her attention to the head and face. Putting her nose close to the dead woman's part-open mouth, she caught the unmistakable, faint reek of Scotch whisky – some of it, or all of it, undoubtedly of her own hospitable providing, she thought ruefully.

And then – slowly, almost with reluctance; the way a cat will approach a saucer of cream: mistrustful, yet knowing all the time that there can be no mistake, not the slightest possible snag – she examined the face – and most particularly the lips and the membranes of the eyes.

She was still looking, and pondering, when there a knock upon the door and Police Constable Tuttle came in, preceded by a bulky man in unseasonable tweeds and a flat cap.

'Doctor May, this is Detective Inspector Wainhouse,' announced the former.

'Found a dead body, eh?' said the man in tweeds. 'Turned out to be a regular busman's holiday for you, hasn't it, Doctor?'

His manner matched his expression, which was supercilious to the point of open contempt – admixed with a blatant air of male chauvinism that made Tina's hackles rise on the instant. Nevertheless, having come across that kind of thing often enough in her particular discipline, she determined – as usual – to brush it aside and get on with the job.

'There are several quite serious anomalies,' she said, indicating the corpse, 'but I may find perfectly satisfactory explanations during the formal autopsy. On the other hand, I may not. In which case, one will have to look for other explanations for. . . .'

'The local police surgeon will be conducting the autopsy,' declared Detective Inspector Wainhouse flatly. 'He's been informed, and a van's coming to conduct the body to the mortuary.'

Tina quenched an impulse to make a sharp riposte to the announcement, considering the brusque – not to say rude – manner in which it had been delivered; but she restrained herself. Instead, she nodded and said: 'Well, in that case, I'd better accompany the van, and point out a few things to the police surgeon that I noticed during. . . .'

'That won't be necessary!' interposed the insufferable Wainhouse. 'Our surgeon's quite capable and qualified to carry out a post mortem.' He sniffed. 'Even if he isn't a TV star.'

In response to that studied insult Tina gathered up her stethoscope, her rubber gloves and a magnifying glass, put them in her attaché case and closed the lid with an air of finality.

'Then I will leave you, Mr Wainhouse,' she said. 'No doubt you will wish to interview me about the other matter when you are less busily engaged.'

'No doubt,' he sneered. 'But I'll deal with the important matter on hand first.'

Tina turned to go, but paused at the door. Eyeing him, she said: 'The police surgeon will undoubtedly arrive at the conclusion that the woman fell in and was drowned, but there are a couple of significant points to be taken into account – one of which will interest you particularly.'

'Oh, yes?' he said, narrowing his eyes at her. 'And what's that?'

'When I removed the swimsuit to examine the surface of the torso,' replied Tina, 'I noticed that it had been put on

63

inside out. The small white gusset at the crutch was on the outside. Now, I only met Mrs Wakeley on one occasion, but she struck me very forcibly as a woman very meticulous over her wearing apparel.

'You will, no doubt, draw your own conclusions, Mr Wainhouse.'

He snatched up the swimsuit from the table, where it lay beside the body, and examined it; his eyes were still narrowed, hot and angry, when he regarded Tina again.

'It's the right way out now!' he grated.

'Naturally,' responded Tina. 'It came the right way out when I peeled it off the body.'

'How do I know?' he growled. 'How do I know you've got it right? You could have got it – all mixed up in your mind!' And he bared his nicotine-stained teeth in a mirthless grin.

The implication was as clear as it was brutal. Tina felt her cheeks grow pale. She made no reply – but spun round on her heel and went out.

On the basis that life must go on, Tina went shopping for provisions after she had left the holiday camp and returned to Clifftop, calling in at the general store and giving an order for various perishable groceries to augment the contents of the deep freeze. Penlee the owner and his wife – a buttoned-up-looking little woman cut from the same bolt of cloth as her spouse – knew full well the identity of the new visitor at Clifftop, but gave no sign of doing so; took her order, promised that the boy would deliver the provisions before noon, and went back to their tasks in a manner which gave Tina the very forcible impression that their eyes would be following her, and their comments coming thick and fast, as soon as she was out of the door.

The rest of the long morning dragged interminably. Ducking away from a recurring impulse metaphorically to cry on someone's shoulder, she deliberately avoided ringing

64

Maggie, Heymans, Derek Arkwright at Scotland Yard, or even – a long shot – her friend and solicitor Janet Barden. Let the situation develop, she told herself; best see how the insufferable Wainhouse handled the disputed issue of the severed head before she started to marshal her forces in support. In this reasoning, she was also being true to her motive for coming down to Cornwall, which was to find herself again – and that, in her stern philosophy, meant standing on her own two feet.

She had not long to wait for her next encounter with the detective inspector: no sooner had she washed up the plates and dishes after her modest lunch than the sound of a car at the top of the lane, followed by a peremptory double knock, announced the arrival of the Law.

'Do come in,' she said with as much *savoir-faire* as she could muster.

Wainhouse had PC Tuttle with him (to see fair play?) and the pair of them refused her offer of coffee, nor would they sit down. The plain-clothes detective took up a proprietorial stance by the fireplace, with feet astride, hands clasped behind his back, head thrust aggressively forward – and addressed his hostile glance towards the image of the Devil punching his way in through the far wall.

'The sort of stuff – I wouldn't call it Art, myself – that takes your fancy, is it, Doctor?' he demanded. And Tina, who would as lief campaign for the return of public hanging as stick up for the paintings of Ellis Duke, found herself doing just that – to her intense annoyance, and in a didactic manner that made her wince with shame:

'There's no denying the artist's sincerity of intention,' she said, 'nor can one close one's mind to his devastating competence.'

Wainhouse glanced sidelong at her, close-set eyes contemplating; it was a full half minute before he responded: 'Done by a feller named Duke,' he said.

'That's right,' said Tina. 'The late Ellis Duke.'

'Killed himself.' The detective nodded – across the room,

southwards and seawards. 'Out there. I handled the case. We never found his body.'

'So I believe,' murmured Tina.

'Mad.'

'It's a much-maligned term,' said Tina, 'but you could put it that way.'

'Friend of' – she had a clear impression that he was only pretending to search for the name – 'that Doctor Heymans, the head-shrinker who often used to appear on TV – like you do.'

'Duke rented the cottage from Doctor Heymans, certainly.'

'Is Doctor Heymans a friend of yours, too – Doctor?'

'Yes.'

'And you're also – like Duke was – a patient of his?'

Tina felt the trap close in about her. Seated as she was, in an easy chair before her interrogator, her hands on her lap, she instinctively drove the fingernails of her clenched hands deeply against the palms – and knew on the instant that Wainhouse had seen the movement, and had figured out the cause.

'Not exactly – a patient,' she said.

He assumed an unconvincing expression of surprise. 'Ah, but I gathered from the press that you were receiving psychiatric treatment from Heymans,' he said, and looked sly.

Tina felt herself on safer ground. 'I had dinner with Dr Heymans,' she said. 'Some nosey-parker saw us together and no doubt telephoned the earth-shaking news to the *Sunday Courier*. That piece of hard fact, added to a couple of other totally innocuous and unconnected items of trivial gossip – well shaken up and with a dash of spice added – amounts to what passes for news in that part of the Fleet Street gutter occupied by your favourite newspaper, Mr Wainhouse.' She smiled sweetly, heartened to see that her riposte had struck home.

His heavy, sullen face flushed unbecomingly. 'That's as may be,' he replied at length. 'But it provides one explanation for the so-called severed head. Something happened to scare you' – he gestured towards the lifelike mural on the far wall – 'Old Nick over there, f'rinstance. And you imagined the rest.

'If you can think of a better explanation for the sudden arrival and disappearance of a head in a box, I'd like to hear it.' He folded his arms with the air of a man who has said all there is to be said. And PC Tuttle nodded fawning agreement with his senior. 'Nevertheless,' he added, 'I'm bound to take note of your complaint, as given to PC Tuttle, here, and set down by him in writing. And I will inquire into the matter.

'Unless,' he added, 'you are willing to withdraw the allegation. In which case – I am empowered to inform you – the matter will be closed, and all records expunged.'

'All records expunged' – she almost laughed aloud at the stilted officialese. Oh, yes, they'll burn the records, all right, and the matter will be closed – except that everyone in Trepoll Haven who doesn't already know about it will know about it next week, followed by the remainder of the West Country, and then all Britain.

'I've nothing to withdraw, Mr Wainhouse,' she said. 'What I saw, I saw. What came and went, came and went.'

He exhaled a long, slow breath. 'Very well, Doctor. You've made your bed, and you must lie in it, as they say. Let's go, Constable. We're wasting our time here. Good afternoon to you, Doctor May.'

She saw them out. One thing remained to be asked:

'Has the police surgeon carried out the post mortem?'

'He has,' replied Wainhouse, opening the car door.

'With what result?'

'Doctor Cobb certified Death by Drowning.'

'Accidental?'

'Of course,' replied Wainhouse, simulating surprise. 'What else?'

'Did he not take into account the fact of the swimsuit being inside out – and other factors?'

'I don't question the work of a professional expert duly appointed to assist the police,' responded the detective,

67

throwing a leg inside the car and settling himself in the driving seat. 'That was Doctor Cobb's conclusion, and there the matter rests.'

He drove away without another glance. Through the rear window of the car Tina could see the two men commenting to each other. And they were both laughing.

Tina checked out the police surgeon in the local phone book. As she had anticipated, he was a general practitioner who presumably did police work under contract:

> Cobb Dr T.O, Physn & Surg–
> Grandison Ho, Truro Rd, St Costello (Residence
> & Practice) .... *St Costello* 518949

She rang the number and a woman answered: a woman with a vibrant contralto voice. Posing as a potential patient, she asked if the doctor could fit her into his evening surgery? Yes, he could, and she would be the last on the list. Eight o'clock. Name, please? Tina gave her name as May – just that.

It was fair to suppose that Cobb would not wish to discuss his post-mortem findings, and, indeed, might have been warned off her by the obnoxious Wainhouse. However, she now had an appointment, and the worst he could do was to ask her to leave when she started throwing questions.

From Heymans' list she got the number of the village taxi service, which was run by a Miss Nancy Chambers, who answered the phone and expressed willingness to take Doctor May to St Costello in time for her appointment at eight o'clock.

She had hardly put the phone back on its rest before it rang out. Scotland Yard on the line – and was Doctor May available to speak to Detective Superintendent Arkwright, please?

Yes, she was – like a shot!

'Tina!'

'Derek – how nice.'

'Tina, how are you? I've been worried about you.'

'Ah, you've been reading the gutter press!'

'That, also. But I don't believe everything I read in the *Sunday Courier*, not by any means. No, Tina, I really rang you to ask about this General Circulation Telex we had in this morning, concerning – of all things – a severed head. And alleged to have been found by you. What's it all about?'

She told him – everything . . . .

'I see,' said Derek Arkwright, when she had finished. 'Well, I don't know what to say, Tina. The local boys will put it through the usual channels – but I didn't get the impression from the telex – and what you've told me confirms it – that they're taking the matter anything like seriously.'

'In short terms,' said Tina, 'the *Courier* has convinced them that I'm a nut-case and that I made the whole thing up. Do *you* think I made the whole thing up, Derek?'

'Idiot!' chuckled Arkwright. 'But, seriously, the matter can't possibly be resolved unless – A – they find the head again, or a body with or without a head to fit it, or – B – someone is reported missing, and you're able to identify him from a photograph as the missing head. In either of those events, the locals might be persuaded to call in the Yard, and I could send Turner down to Cornwall right away and I could follow as soon as he's on to something.'

'Oh, Derek, it's such a comfort to know I've got you to back me up. This thing had really begun to get me down. I had a Detective Inspector Wainhouse round here just now, and he was pressurizing me to recant my story.'

'It's not the kind of case that much appeals to a hard-working local tec. Promises a lot of footwork and probably nothing to show at the end of it. I take it you didn't recant?'

'I did not!'

'Good for you – and very typical.' Arkwright chuckled. 'Well, I've got a bit of local pull with the deputy chief constable of the Duchy, who used to be my chief here. Best if a bit of pressure's applied, to make them clear it up. An unsubstantiated – and unresolved – allegation of that sensational nature isn't going to do your career any good.'

'I'd thought of that, too,' said Tina.

'Well, apart from that, how're you getting on down there?'

'Fine. Rushed off my feet. Apart from the severed head, I'm also involved in a drowning. They say it's by accident, but someone will have to clear up a couple of points before I'm convinced she wasn't pushed.'

Arkwright laughed aloud at that. And on this note of gallows' humour, they parted.

'The great Doctor May! Oh, this is an honour – and a real pleasure!'

This from Miss Nancy Chambers, who arrived outside the cottage in her taxi at a quarter to eight. Diminutive, sharp-featured, fifty-ish, her hair touched up with henna and dressed in two coils, like earphones over each ear, she exuded an indefinable air of the kind of earnestness that was more suited to decades gone past.

'I've watched your programmes,' she continued. 'Every one. And I mustn't forget to ask you to write in my autograph book.'

(Also a very straightforward person: in nine cases out of ten, fans usually claimed that they were demanding one's autograph on behalf of a friend or relation who went in for such silly affectations.)

'It will be a pleasure,' said Tina.

The car was an old but well-kept $1\frac{1}{2}$-litre Riley, and Miss Chambers drove it with meticulous care down the rutted lane, out into the village street and up the road signposted: St Costello 3m. Tina noticed that she was wearing very professional-looking driving gloves, the sort they wear on rallies – and deduced from this and the rest of the available evidence that Trepoll Haven's taxi service was in the hands of a car enthusiast.

70

'She's pinking a bit on the up-gradient,' said Miss Chambers. 'The old dear needs a decoke. A bit like her owner.' And that took care of the car-enthusiast theory – and her sense of humour.

'Shall you want me to bring you back, Doctor?' she asked.

'That would be very convenient,' said Tina. 'Trouble is, I don't know whether I shall be there for ten seconds – or for the rest of the evening. It depends.'

'The ten-second wait's no problem,' said the other. 'I'll stick around if it's going to be as short a time as that. Trouble is, I've got another job at eight-thirty – a trip to Mevagissey and back. Best thing you can do is ring my sister at our address when your appointment's over and you're ready to come back. Or else you could pick up a taxi in St Costello.'

'I'll contact your number when I'm finished,' said Tina.

Her driver nodded agreement, and busied herself with the task of crossing over the main east-west highway that ran parallel with the coast a mile at the back of the village. There was a lot of holiday traffic moving westwards: family cars with roofs piled high with camping gear; caravans and giant touring coaches. Miss Chambers carefully stayed put at the double white line till she saw a long gap in the passing queues and slipped neatly over the crossroads.

'How do you like Clifftop, Doctor?' she asked. And Tina met her eyes in the rear-view mirror: they were distinctly watchful.

'Very comfortable,' she replied. And because there seemed no point in beating about the bush, for this woman – taxi driver in a small rural community – almost certainly knew all that had happened to her since she arrived, probably even knew the colour of her pyjamas, she added: 'I could have done without some of the excitement and upset, though.'

'Yes, it was a terrible pity about Mrs Wakeley,' replied the other. 'Such a super person. Full of life. It's hard to think of her dying like that. She was a fantastically good swimmer. Must have hit her head on the bottom, do you think?' It was a direct question: the eyes were fixed on her again.

71

'It's a rational explanation,' replied Tina non-committally.

'The vicar will be lost without her,' said Miss Chambers. 'Poor old chap. He was supposed to be retiring at the end of the year, and they were going to live in a farmhouse that Mrs Wakeley owned in the south of France. I don't suppose the poor old feller will fancy going there on his own.

'Mind you,' she went on, 'I can't say as I approved of all the things as Mrs Wakeley used to get up to when that Ellis Duke was alive. Disgusting carryings-on, if you ask me.'

'You mean the – *coven*?' asked Tina, drawing a bow at a venture.

'That's what they called it,' said her informant. 'And still do. Disgusting. Mind you, I should be the last one to throw stones, since my own kith and kin, my own sister Meg, was part of it. Oh, yes, Meg was into it – the wild parties up at Clifftop, bathing orgies down on the beach. Beats me why the police never moved in and stopped them – well, to tell you the truth, there's no mystery why they didn't.' She was silent for a while as they came into the outskirts of St Costello – market town, light industrial centre, seat of local government and heart of the area – and negotiated a flower-bedecked roundabout.

'Was Ellis Duke a friend of yours, Doctor?' she then asked. 'If he was, I've really put my foot in it.'

'I never knew him,' said Tina. 'Doctor Heymans is a friend of mine, but he only knew Duke as a patient and someone to whom he rented the cottage.'

'We don't see much of Doctor Heymans,' said Miss Chambers. 'Pity. He used to make me laugh on that programme he had. A very funny man.'

'Yes,' agreed Tina, and, probing: 'Tell me more about the coven, Miss Chambers. 'How did your sister come to join, since – as I take it – you don't approve of such goings-on yourself?'

'My sister Meg,' replied the other, 'now she represents what you might call the young set of Trepoll, for all that she's in her forties. We don't have any young people in the village,

72

you see? There's nothing for them. The young married couples who have babies, they've all moved out here to St Costello, or elsewhere, to live where the work is.

'There's nothing left in Trepoll but a bit of crab and lobster fishing for the old fellers. The villagers of Meg's age – those who're looking for a spot of high life – they mix with what we call "the foreigners": the weekend cottagers from London, and the artists and writers of Ellis Duke's sort. The sort that made up the coven.

'I should say "*make* up" the coven – for it didn't go away when Ellis Duke died.'

'Is it still in operation, then?' asked Tina, thinking of the murals, particularly the one of the seashore orgy; remembering also – for reasons she could only half imagine – the severed head that had stared up at her from the kitchen table. . . .

'It is,' replied Miss Chambers, 'and I'll tell you all about it, but that'll have to wait for now, 'cos we're here. This is Doctor Cobb's place. Do you know him? No? Oh, you'll like Doctor Cobb. I wish he had a surgery in Trepoll, instead of that old fogey we've got there.' She drew to a halt at the gates of an impressive-looking Edwardian house standing in its own grounds, with a handsome, formal garden set with rose beds, well-matured monkey puzzle trees and the ubiquitous sub-tropical palms of southern Cornwall.

It was two minutes to the hour. 'Will you wait for me a little while, then?' asked Tina.

'I can give you five minutes, and then I'd best be back. But you ring Meg when you want me to pick you up.'

'All right. Thanks, Miss Chambers.' Tina got out of the car and shut the door.

The woman leaned forward across the passenger seat and looked earnestly up at her.

'On the way back,' she said, 'I'll fill you in on a lot of things about Trepoll.

'See you later, Doctor.'

Five

Once inside the gates and half-way down the drive, Tina saw a woman by the side of the house. She was cutting roses from a well-laden bush and laying them carefully in a trug at her feet. She paused when she heard Tina's footfalls crunch on the gravel, but did not look round.

'Is that Doctor May?' she called out.

'Yes,' responded Tina, surprised at being so addressed.

'I'm Anna Cobb,' said the other, picking up the trug. 'My son will be just about ready for you. Come on inside.' And she set off to walk across the lawn to meet Tina about half-way towards the front porch of the house. 'Isn't it a simply lovely evening?' she said.

'It's been a wonderful summer so far,' responded Tina.

The other was sixty-plus: grey-haired, blue-eyed; dressed in a print overall, sensible shoes, gardening gloves. The sonorous contralto voice was the one Tina had heard on the phone. As if she had read her companion's thought, the other woman said: 'I recognized your voice from the TV – and, of course, we'd already heard on the grape vine that you were staying at Trepoll. This way, please.'

It was cool and shadowy inside the house; somewhere a long-case clock ticked ponderously, and the pleasant scent of lavender floor polish faintly pervaded all.

Tina's guide opened a door marked *Waiting Room* and stood aside to let her pass through. It was not furnished, like so many of its kind, with tables littered with National Health Service hand-outs, odd copies of *Punch* and *Country Life*, nor were there posters relating to health and hygiene pinned around the walls; instead, the flavour was that of an upper-middle-class sitting room in a country-town house. The furnishings were late Victorian, simple, comfortable. There were watercolours and oils of vaguely theatrical subjects around the walls, one of which particularly took Tina's attention: it showed a woman in seventeenth-century costume standing against a stage backdrop of a wooded park; given the passage of twenty years or so, it had to represent her companion in her young prime. A former actress: that would account for the beautiful voice.

Feeling called upon to make some comment, Tina said: 'It's a very good likeness, I recognized you at once.'

'Recognized me?' The woman turned to face her, and the blue eyes wavered unsteadily in her direction, settling upon a spot somewhere well to one side. 'Oh, you mean the picture. . . .'

Any further communication was averted by the ring of a bell coming from beyond a communicating door.

'You can go in now, Doctor May,' said the blind woman.

'Good evening, Doctor May.'

A figure rose from behind an old-fashioned roll-top desk. 'Brown' should have been Cobb's family name, for it would have suited him admirably: brown hair and eyes, ruddy-brown complexion; even the lightweight, double-breasted town suit in which his tall and powerful frame was clothed was of a formal subfusc. And he possessed a deep-brown and extremely pleasant voice – presumably a legacy of the actress mother.

'Nice of you to see me,' said Tina, extending her hand, which he took in his. 'Particularly since, as you must have realized by now, I don't come as a patient.'

'You come about the post mortem,' he supplied. And Tina had a clear impression that he was suppressing a smile.

'Detective Inspector Wainhouse has warned you against me!' she cried.

It was not a smile, but a grin – and a broad one – that lit up his bronzed, open, countryman's face like a lamp. 'Yes, Wainhouse is a bit of a pain,' he said, 'but I don't necessarily jump when he says "Jump". And I really would like to talk to you about that drowning case.' He indicated an easy chair for her to sit in, and went over to a cabinet which, upon being opened, revealed itself as a refrigerator containing bottles and glasses. 'What'll you have to drink? Just name it.'

Armed with a Scotch, she watched him open a bottle of stout and pour the contents into a pewter tankard.

'When they told me you'd been first on the scene and had taken a look around,' he said, 'I had a notion that you'd query my findings. Cheers!'

'Your very good health,' said Tina. 'In short, I don't see how you can blithely dismiss it as accidental drowning – by the way, it *was* asphyxiation by drowning, I take it – not suffocation?'

'Drowned,' confirmed Cobb. 'Someone had pounded out most of the water, but the lungs still reeked of chlorine and assorted pool chemicals.'

'There were the bruises,' she said.

'I took those into account.'

'I concede that the one on the head could have been either from the edge of the pool, or from striking the bottom,' said Tina. 'But those on the wrists and forearm. . . .'

He nodded. 'I take your point. But the issue's still open. I noted the bruises in my report, but drew no conclusions about the arm and wrists. If Wainhouse comes up with any further, non-medical, evidence before the inquest that goes any way to explaining the bruises, the coroner will act accordingly, and. . . .'

Tina, who had been fairly writhing with suppressed impatience while Cobb had been talking, could not restrain herself from interposing:

'Wainhouse isn't interested in any further evidence! As far as he's concerned, it's accidental drowning. Why – he totally dismissed my point about the swimsuit!'

Cobb looked puzzled. 'What swimsuit?' he asked.

'God! Don't tell me he didn't even mention it to you?' cried Tina.

'No, he didn't. Tell me about it.'

So she told him.

When she had finished doing so, he picked up the phone.

'Mother,' he said, 'will you please take any incoming calls and see that Doctor May and I are not disturbed? Thanks, dear.'

From where she was sitting, Tina could see through the long window of the surgery to the driveway, the gates, and the street beyond.

Miss Chambers had gone back to Trepoll Haven.

'No, Wainhouse never breathed a word to me about the swimsuit anomaly,' said Cobb. 'And, since I've now met you and formed my own opinion, and because, as every man in the street knows, we of the medical persuasion stick together through thick and thin, I will add that he thinks you are out of your mind.'

'Do you think I'm out of my mind?' she asked. And recalled that this was more or less the same challenge she had put to Derek Arkwright a few hours previously.

The brown eyes panned over her. 'No, I don't,' replied Cobb. 'But I'd say you've been under a lot of strain recently. Are you sleeping badly?'

'Mmmm.'

'Taking anything for it?'

She named the particular brand of barbiturate that she had prescribed for herself, and the dosage.

'That's a bit over the top,' opined Cobb. 'I've found better results with the benzodiazepines in low dosage, and I'll give you some before you leave. Are you driving? If not, you can have a refill.'

'Taxi.'

'Have a refill.' He took her glass. 'And give it me, from the top, exactly how you see Mrs Wakeley *not* being accidentally drowned.' He paused at the fridge. 'By the way – do you have a particular fancy for who might have done it?'

Tina shook her head.

'Right.' He handed back her recharged glass. 'From the top. Her car arrives in the holiday camp car park some time around – say – eight o'clock, maybe earlier. But no one saw it arrive, and it was still there after she'd been fished out of the pool.'

'She was unconscious,' said Tina. 'Unconscious from a blow on the temple which she had tried to avoid. In the course of the struggle, her assailant had grabbed hold of her wrist and arm. Maybe he got a good purchase, eventually, on her right forearm, and this enabled him to strike her across the left temple with whatever he used as a blunt instrument.'

'This wasn't in the car park, by the pool, anywhere in the holiday camp?' interpolated Cobb.

'No,' said Tina. 'That would invalidate my theory about the swimsuit. It has to be somewhere else. At her home – or whatever she spent the night.'

'Her lover's place?'

'Don't let's assume too much at this stage. Anyhow, she probably wasn't dressed when it happened. Possibly in a nightdress. . . .'

'So she's lying there unconscious,' supplied Cobb. 'He knows she swims at the camp every fine morning in summer. So he puts her into her swimsuit – which she has with her, for the morning. . . .'

'In his hurry, he puts it on inside out.'

'Being a man, he probably wouldn't notice anyhow.'

'And then he drives her to the holiday camp,' said Tina. 'Wearing a mackintosh over the swimsuit – it was found scrumpled up beside the pool!'

'Carries her round there. . . .'

'Lowers her in – face-first. . . .'

'She inhales water, still unconscious. . . .'

Cobb sat back in his office chair. 'I'll buy it,' he said.

The phone rang.

'Mother, dear, is it very important?' he asked into the mouthpiece. Tina saw his expression change at the muted reply.

'Good God!' he said, and put the instrument down.

'What happened?' asked Tina.

'That was the police,' he said. 'There's been an accident on the St Costello road. Your village taxi driver. . . .'

'Miss Chambers!'

'You know her? Well – of course you must.'

'She drove me here!' cried Tina. 'It must have happened on her way back. Is she – badly hurt?'

Cobb was already snatching up his bag. 'They didn't say. Just called for me to go along there.' The dark brown eyes fixed her gaze for a moment. 'Coming too, Doctor May?'

The police had flashing signs out, Go Slow notices, and a motorcycle patrolman was shepherding traffic along one side of the road. The southbound lane was taken up by the 1½-litre Riley which had apparently gone straight through a gentle bend instead of round it and had ended up against a pollarded willow tree close by the verge. The car was minus its front offside wheel. All the doors were open. A small knot of people was grouped around the supine figure of a woman lying with her skirt rucked up to show the tops of woollen stockings. There was an ambulance parked on the verge just round the bend. A uniformed para-medic was kneeling beside the victim.

Tina drew breath sharply to see the livid face pillowed against a red blanket – and instinctively knew herself to be in the threatening presence of that grim figure, Death, whom she feared above all.

'How is she?' asked Cobb.

The ambulance man glanced up at him, his young face full of strain.

'I think she's going, Doctor,' he whispered. 'Just given her morphine. She spoke a few words a while back.'

Tina and her companion knelt each side of the stricken woman, whose eyes were part-open and gazing sightlessly up at the trees and sky. Her hands were folded over the edge of the blanket that covered her, and the very white fingers – white and curiously small, already, like those of the dead – were plucking feebly at the woollen material.

The pale lips moved, causing a thin trickle of bright blood to emerge from the corner of the mouth and be lost in the red blanket.

'She's saying something again,' whispered the ambulance man.

Cobb had taken one of the limp hands in his two hands and was stroking it gently; he leaned forward, close by the grey curl of plait that masked one ear.

'Are you in pain, Nancy?' he said. 'I'm Doctor Cobb.'

The eyelids flickered wide. Tina thought she saw the wraith of a smile touch the pale lips.

'Doc–tor. . . .'

'Made a bit of a mess of yourself, Nancy,' said Cobb.

'The – the wheel. . . .'

'Wheel came off, did it? Bad thing to happen, Nancy. What was that you said?'

The pale lips were fighting frantically to issue sound and meaning; Cobb bent his head closer, till his cheek was all but touching hers.

'I didn't quite get that, Nancy,' he said. 'Something about – yes – tell Doctor May – tell Doctor May what, Nancy?'

Tina clenched her hands tightly and held her breath. All she could see of Nancy Chambers' face, which was part-hidden by Cobb's head, was the frantic mouth, now fast losing connection with the will that directed it. She thought she heard her name repeated again – and then the movement stilled.

Cobb straightened up.

'She's gone,' he murmured, and passing a hand across the dead face he closed the unseeing eyes for ever.

'Did you catch anything she said?' asked Tina.

He shook his head. 'There was something she wanted to tell you very badly,' he said, and he looked across the still form and searched her out. ' "Tell Doctor May," she said, over and over again – but whatever it was, she was never able to get it out, poor thing.' Tenderly, he covered the new corpse with a blanket and stood up. Hardly had he done so when a police car slewed to a halt close by, blue lamp flashing, and tweed-clad Wainhouse got out. His close-set eyes took in the scene of the shrouded corpse by the roadside, Tina and Cobb standing side by side, the attendant police.

'How did it happen, then?' he demanded. 'Anybody know? Were there any witnesses?'

Working on the fatal front offside wheel, one of the police officers had prised off the hub cap and found something lying inside it. This he held out in his hand for the detective to see: it was a single, octagonal-shaped nut.

'There's your answer, Mr Wainhouse, sir,' he said. 'Somebody unscrewed three of the nuts, loosened this one, then put the hub cap back on. It only took a shortish run for this single nut to work its way right off the retaining bolt.'

It seemed to Tina that a cold finger trailed slowly down the entire length of her spine. She shuddered.

'I reckon you've got it just about right,' replied Wainhouse. He turned to Tina and bared his teeth in a sour grimace. 'Another death, eh, Doctor? The place has never been the same since you came.'

Tom Cobb offered to drive her somewhere for dinner, but she thanked him and took a rain check on the offer, so he gave her a lift back to the cottage, and she was glad of his company when he went in with her and – without being asked – walked through all the rooms and made sure that the windows and doors had not been tampered with.

As he said: 'Let's face it. We've got a killer around this place, and he came very close to you this evening: that wheel

81

could have just as likely come off a couple of miles earlier on. Can't be too careful – and watchful.'

On an impulse, Tina then told him about the severed head. Cobb listened with grave concern, and assured her that Wainhouse had not confided in him about the matter, nor was he able to shed any light on the identity of the head or put forward any ideas as to the mystery donor. He then returned to the theme of the undoubtedly murdered taxi driver – it being of more immediate, pressing significance.

'What puzzles me,' he said, 'is who in heaven would want to harm a simple, uncomplicated soul like poor Nancy Chambers? She never went further than Plymouth in all her life, nor ever did anything more sensational than have a rather flighty sister.'

It was then that Tina, while pouring him a drink, gave Cobb a brief run-down of her conversation with the dead woman, ending with Nancy Chambers' cryptic pronouncement upon their parting company. 'Is it likely that Nancy had something on someone?' she concluded, 'and she was – quite simply – silenced on that account?'

'Quite likely,' responded Cobb. 'But it would be a waste of time trying to sell the idea to Wainhouse – and, by the way, that was an outrageous remark he made to you back there, even if it was only intended as what he would consider to be a wisecrack.'

'Thanks for rebuking him, for all that,' said Tina. 'Coming on top of having to watch that woman die, it was just about the last straw to hear that I was somehow to blame – even if only by association.'

He swallowed the last of his drink and stood up. 'You look absolutely wrung out,' he said. 'I'll buzz off so you can get an early night. And don't forget to take one of the sleepers I gave you.'

'I won't,' said Tina. 'Thanks.'

She watched him drive away into the gathering gloom, and experienced a sudden sense of panic at the thought of being alone. This she very sensibly combated by taking a walk

82

around the outside of the cottage to reassure herself that nothing had changed since the sunlight had lit upon every flower's head, every wavelet, roof and headland. Sunset accomplishes nothing, save to shroud the intensity of seeing. Everything still remains; it is only the thought of what might be *added* that accounts for the dread of night.

So she must see for herself that nothing alien had come to threaten her well-being, and that the small garden, and the wasteland of gorse and pine beyond its boundary, were just as they had been in the daylight.

She stayed outside for a little while, watching the last of the sunlight die behind the far headland, throwing it into sharp definition, as it also did to the nearer finger of rock that masked the pathway to the village – where she had met the Reverend Arthur Wakeley, now a widower.

She wondered how he was taking it. And, remembering how he had struck her so forcibly as a man afraid, felt certain that the old man must surely be taking his vivacious wife's death very badly indeed. She decided that – out of creature compassion if nothing else – she would call on him and offer her personal condolences. Oddly fortified by this good resolution, Tina went back into the cottage and rustled up something for supper before an early bed.

Alas, for an early bed. . . .

For a start, her tiredness seemed to have worn off. This may have been due to the walk around in the fresh air.

She ate a surprisingly hearty supper of bread and cheese and pickles, washed down with a glass of a robust red table wine, followed by a cup of strong coffee. Over this, she skimmed the newspaper which, offering nothing by way of either instruction or entertainment, she soon exchanged for Dickens. The saga of Sydney Carton also failed for once to capture her interest and attention, so – still restless – she manufactured the excuse of tidying up the place a little, and walked around with a feather duster.

It was by then past eleven-thirty.

The bookcase in the study still made a good job of masking the worst of the sacrifice mural; it was a pity that she was unable to contrive something to hide the one in the bathroom. Perhaps she might follow Dermot Heymans' suggestion and whitewash it over?

She sat on the edge of the bath and studied the composition. While at first glance the seascape with figures appeared to depict a cheerful nude romp in the open air – a Boucher, or even a Böcklin – decided overtones of menace soon obtruded. It might be her imagination, thought Tina, but surely the satanic figure was staring down at the complaisant naiad imprisoned in his encircling arm with something more than simple lust; wasn't there more than a hint of – cruelty – in the pale eye, in the curve of the goatish lips? And the mermaid who was floating just beneath the surface in the foreground above the bath, her moist eyes wide and staring like submerged oysters – was she alive, or dead? That whole, soundless company of roistering demon-worshippers – why – they put her in mind of a pictorial image that had once disgusted yet curiously allured her: the portrayal of a section of the vast audience at a Roman 'games': men and women, both, satiated with the common-place vices and discovering their true release in the shedding of blood.

It was then that Tina saw the artist's intent: the mural represented some kind of ritual bath, a communal cleansing in preparation for – what?

Harking back to the scene on the study wall – *a sacrifice?* . . .

There was no sleep for her. She took another glass of wine, tried her book again but found it unsatisfying, paced restlessly up and down the sitting room till she heard the distant chimes of midnight ring out from St Botolph's church down in the village, and caught the reply from a tower or steeple in a distant parish.

As if summoned, she snatched up a walking stick and went out into the night.

*

From the clifftop she could see the whole sweep of the bay and its attendant lights: the glow from cottage windows fronting the harbour; a dull glimmer from an isolated farmstead on the heights towards St Costello; the brilliant beam of the lighthouse on the point as it fingered the horizon of ships that carried pinpoints of red, green and white; and, near at hand, the lambent glow of fireflies weaving a complicated figure around a gorse bush.

Tina opened a rickety gate that led out on to the clifftop waste and set off towards the west.

The part which auto-suggestion played in the episode that followed, or how the traumas of the day might have subscribed towards it, or the heady wine she had taken with her supper, or – and it remained forever the least acceptable factor in the mental equation – how her supposed 'nervous breakdown' could have been the decisive factor – none of this was she ever afterwards able to resolve.

The fact was – it happened. . . .

It began with a faint glow in the sky: a loom of ruddy light that sprang to being above the finger of rock which descended across the beach to the shoreline. As she drew closer, it became apparent that the source was a bonfire: every so often, a shower of bright sparks rose, like the fireflies of the clifftop, above the crest of the rock – as if someone had stirred the fire below.

Nearer still, Tina slowed her pace and instinctively lightened her tread, though her footfalls made scarcely any sound in the thick mat of dead moss and pine needles that carpeted her way.

Presently the sound of shrill voices brought her to a halt. Straining her ears, she heard wild laughter, a woman's screech, the bass roar of rumbustious men at horseplay. And, though her will fought against it, her curiosity directed her dragging footsteps forward again.

The glow of the bonfire presently lit up the cliff face, and the sounds grew louder and more explicit. When she reached the rock wall that shut the merrymakers from her sight, Tina dropped to her hands and knees and crept forward the last few yards, still clutching tightly her walking stick. Now she could hear the crackle of burning wood, and even the surge of spent surf among the broken rocks at the end of the miniature headland.

A foot from her goal, she bowed her head and closed her eyes, took a deep breath to steady herself – then, slowly and with infinite caution, she peered over the sharp edge of the col which descended seawards to the beach; and saw what was taking place in the sandy amphitheatre below.

The bonfire was quite small, but was enough to light up sand, shingle, cliff and surf for a wide radius. It illuminated a group of a dozen or so people who circled it, hands joined, casting their grotesquely elongated shadows as far as its loom extended, so that the very cliff wall was peopled with capering giant figures.

From her high vantage point Tina was too far away to distinguish their faces; all she could do was single out male from female – and this because they were all stark naked.

They were mouthing some kind of chant – a repetitive mantra that was forever pierced with shrieks of laughter as one or other of the sexes seized hold of a near neighbour and subjected him or her to a rough embrace, while occasionally they broke off in ones and twos to snatch up bottles which were strewn around, and lift them to thirsty lips. . . .

The orgiastic proceedings changed pace with the rise and fall of the fire; frenzy reigned when the flames rose high, and subsided to a kind of lethargy when the pieces of driftwood burned down to glowing embers – mounting yet again when another load was thrown on, and the flames sent sparks flying up into the night sky.

The watcher lay huddled on high, fascinated yet repulsed by the scene below her. She remained there when all of the driftwood had been used up and the flames sank for the last time to a bed of red ash that cast a bloody pall over the circle of nude forms. It was then, in the gathering darkness, that the orgiasts fell silent, sank on their hunkers, pair by pair, in huddled embraces; and seemed to be waiting – with their faces turned towards the incoming sea and the lines of crawling, pale surf. And the keynote was – expectation.

Suddenly one of the party – a tall, male, bearded creature – rose to his feet and, raising his arms above his head, began to chant something in a quavering voice. The hair at the back of Tina's neck stiffened and pricked as the remainder of the gathering took up the rhythm of the chant in an eerie ululation.

Next there was a sudden silence, and the bearded figure pointed to the tip of the small headland, where from out of the tumbled rocks and breaking surf there appeared another figure. And Tina strained her gaze to make out the form and features of the newcomer.

Was he – it was another male – covered all over in hair? In the disturbed night that followed, she asked herself this many times. Did he shamble – *shamble*, there was no other word for it – on goat's feet, and was there tufted hair upon his skinny flanks? And when he came within the compass of the dying fire, did he have the goat face, goat eyes, slackly-open goat's mouth – like the Devil frozen in the act of punching through the wall in Clifftop Cottage?

She never waited to find out, but was on her feet and running, pell-mell – back the way she had come. Nor did she stop till she had flung herself in through the door of the cottage and, throwing herself down into a chair, stared back at the door which she had locked and bolted against the night and all that it held. And wondered how much of what she had witnessed had been reality, and how much the workings of her assaulted mind.

She took Tom Cobb's prescription, but the benzodiazepine

only crumpled the edges of her consciousness, so that she slept in fitful stops and starts, spinning out what was left of the short night into a seeming eternity of disturbing images that lay inside and outside of sleep and in the limbo-land at the middle.

When the thin light of dawn seeped in through the uncurtained windows of her bedroom she crawled out of bed, went downstairs, and ran herself a tepid bath. Then, stripping off her pyjamas, which were sticky with night sweat, she directed her gaze – slowly and hesitantly – towards the cavorting, painted figures all about her.

Yes – what she had witnessed was a fair approximation to the *mise en scène* displayed about the walls: the setting was the same, there was a like number of participants to those she had seen down on the beach; their antics – though taking place in the shallows instead of on dry land – were of the same, abandoned kind. As for the central figure, the goat-man of the satanic leer, she could not quite be sure. . . .

Had she panicked a little too early? Moments later, the figure would have come within the light of the dying fire and she would have known for sure, whether or not her imagination had played her tricks. . . .

Whether or not the sea, which had swallowed up Ellis Duke, had spewed forth the demonic figure of his painting!

This unhealthy line of thought was broken by the sound of the letter box being rattled – or it may have been the front-door knocker. The newspaper delivery was very early today. Even as she slipped on her dressing gown, she thought she could hear footfalls – rapid footfalls – fading off down the lane.

There was no newspaper on the mat. Perhaps today's was an extra-fat edition and he had been unable to push it through the narrow aperture. Then he must have left it tucked under the door knocker – and that would account for the sound she heard.

Tina gave an involuntary yawn as she opened the door: really, she thought, one must get an early night, or this retreat

88

into the peace and quiet of the countryside was going to drive one to a psychiatric ward.

'*Oooooh. . .!*'

What she saw there, hanging from the heavy brass door knocker, made her recoil as if from a vision of hell itself. Backing up against the door jamb, she closed her eyes and deliberately allowed herself the space of five deep breaths before she uttered the shuddering heart-cry:

'Who could *do* this obscene thing to me?'

Six

Eating breakfast was quite out of the question. She did what had to be done with the obscenity on her door, dressed and made herself a cup of black coffee and sat down to think things through again; hardly had she lifted the cup when the phone rang. It was Derek Arkwright.

'Tina, I hear you've had more trouble down there.'

'The car-smash. Yes,' she replied. 'But how does a small item like that reach your ears in Scotland Yard, Derek?'

He gave a grunt. 'Huh! I've arranged for all the Devon and Cornwall Constabulary reports to be passed on to my desk immediately. I see your name featured in this one. Did you know the woman?'

'I'd just been travelling with her. She taxied me to St Costello minutes before she was killed.'

'Did she, by God? Then it could have been. . . .'

'Could have been what, Derek?'

'I'll say no more.'

'What you mean is,' said Tina, 'that the tampering with the wheel could have been intended for me – for some reason I can't fathom. Yes, the thought had passed through my mind.'

'Me also – but that's just my suspicious copper's mind at work. Hell, you haven't been in Trepoll Haven long enough, nor met enough people, surely, to rate as a potential murder victim.'

She said: 'There's someone – or some people – in the district who think sufficiently ill of me to leave an offering at the door this morning which – considering my particular pet hang-up and phobia – means they hate me, but good.'

'Tell me.'

She drew a shuddering breath. 'It was – a bunch of dead

90

snakes! Adders. All tied together with string round their necks. Their mouths all open to show the poison fangs, Derek, and their horrid little eyes open and staring at me. . . .' She broke off, conscious of the note of near-hysteria that had crept into her voice all unbidden.

'And you've got a real snake phobia, eh?'

'I'm terrified of them. You wouldn't believe. And now I've remembered that the gorse on the clifftop is supposed to be crawling with the things. You know? – I once read somewhere that the record for the biggest adder ever found in Britain belongs to Trepoll Haven. I shall never set foot up there on that cliff again – *never!*'

'Take it easy, Tina. We all have our hang-ups. Mine's flying. But, tell me – how could anyone know about yours?'

'I've thought that one out,' she replied. 'I once mentioned it during the *Pathologist* programme, when Toby Jakeman started on about what he sneeringly called "the self-indulgence of phobias".'

'Anyhow, Tina. There's no harm done and you've got rid of the nuisance, I take it?'

'You bet! I lifted them off the door knocker with a pair of fire tongs and carried them at arm's length to a grave I'd dug.

'But it's left me uneasy, Derek. I mean – *who?* . . .'

'I wouldn't take it too seriously,' said Arkwright, 'but it might be a good idea to mention it to the village copper. It was almost certainly the work of mischievous kids. He'll know who – and put a scare into them.'

She said: 'I don't think I'll mention it to PC Tuttle, Derek. Along with his superior officer, he already thinks I'm a nut-case – and he'd put the snake story down to yet another manifestation of my dotty imagination.'

Arkwright let that pass, contenting himself with an admonition that she took care of herself. There was a brief exchange of good wishes. And on that inconclusive note, they rang off.

*

Tina had another visitor within the half-hour. A knock on the front door summoned her to unlock and unbolt – but not before she called out to check who it was. She opened up, to meet the bland face of PC Tuttle, a blandness that was only slightly overlaid with an expression of derision.

'Taking plenty of precautions, eh, Doctor?' he observed.

Tina made no reply to that, but it fortified her resolve to say nothing to him about the adders.

'What can I do for you, Officer?' she asked with as much coolness as she could muster.

'The post mortem on Nancy Chambers has been set for eleven-thirty this morning at St Costello,' he replied. 'And Doctor Cobb rang for me to ask if you'd like to attend and observe? He tried to get you a while back, before he went on his rounds, but your phone was engaged.'

'Yes, I'll come,' said Tina. And then, remembering: 'Oh, but there's no taxi – any longer. . . .'

'A police car will pick you up at eleven-fifteen, Doctor,' said Tuttle, and turned to go. But Tina had a sudden inspiration:

'Oh, Officer – just one thing I meant to ask. . . .'

He looked round. 'Yes?'

'Tell me about the coven.'

'The – what?'

'Coven, Officer,' she repeated. 'Surely you know what that is. The late Mr Duke organized one right here in Trepoll Haven, and Nancy Chambers, when I spoke to her just before she was killed, was quite forthcoming about it.

'Surely you, as the local policeman, must be better informed than most.'

His face was quite guileless – or was it simply buttoned up?

'I've heard tell of such carryings-on,' he conceded. 'Idle gossip about idle folk. The Devil, they say, finds work for idle hands – so why shouldn't he likewise find silly play for the selfsame? Yes, I reckon as how Mr Duke had something of the sort going.'

'And is it still – going?' she asked.

He looked surprised; though, like the guilelessness, that might also have been put on.

'If you was thinking of midnight bathing parties,' he said, 'with stripping off, booze and suchlike carryings-on – there's plenty of that all round the coast. But they're not local folks who're involved. And they're mostly teenagers. Bikers and suchlike layabouts.'

Teenagers, she thought. If in doubt, blame youth – the universal whipping boys.

'Was that all you wanted to ask, Doctor?' he queried.

'That was all, Officer.'

He nodded. 'The police car will pick you up at eleven-fifteen.'

The mortuary was housed in the Cornwall and St Costello District General Hospital, and contained within its complex the pathological department, an up-to-date deep-freeze unit, lavishly equipped examination theatres, showers and changing rooms for staff – everything that Tina May felt the lack of back at the old South-West London mortuary.

Cobb was waiting for her. His white gown accentuated the bronzed sheen of his face, arms and hands. He looked pleased to see her, and she warmed to the thought of having someone with whom she might be able to share the traumas of the previous twelve hours. Derek Arkwright was a dear friend, she told herself, but he was far away and a policeman to boot; she immediately suffered a bad pang of conscience for the unworthy thought.

'How did the sleepers work out?' asked Cobb.

'I'll tell you all about it later,' she replied.

They walked together along an antiseptic-reeking corridor towards a door marked: Keep Out.

'The sister – her name's Meg – is in the waiting room,' he said. 'Since you were the last to speak with Nancy, she not unnaturally wants to talk to you about how she was – what she had to say – and all that. Only. . . .'

93

'Only – what?' asked Tina.

'Well, she's understandably overwrought, so you'll have to make allowances for her rather wild ramblings.'

Tina shrugged. 'Of course.'

A magnificent modern cupola of frosted glass provided daylight lighting in the post-mortem theatre, and there was no shortage of artificial sources. The body of the late Nancy Chambers lay upon a soak-away examination table of extreme complexity: capable of being raised and lowered, tilted in any direction, with a range of work surfaces scaled to the dimensions of the cadaver under examination.

As soon as Tina had robed, Cobb began work. His deftness in opening up the torso from throat to groin with one clean sweep of his scalpel won her admiration. Together they pored over the revealed viscera.

'Ruptured liver,' said Cobb, probing. 'Even if she'd survived, this and a lot more would have meant lifelong invalidism. See that?' He made an incision and a gush of dark blood was released from the chest cavity. 'She took the impact of the entire steering wheel. Was she wearing a seat belt when you were riding with her?'

'I don't remember,' admitted Tina.

Nothing remained but the usual routine checking for drugs, alcohol, any form of physical failure – all negative, though Cobb rigorously took samples for laboratory examination. 'Wasted effort,' was his comment. 'The tampered-with wheel explains all.'

Tina nodded agreement. During the course of his inspection for tell-tale hypodermic punctures, Cobb had extended the dead arms. While he was in the act of laying the left arm straight again, Tina saw something. . . .

'Hold it!' she murmured, and picked up the limb by the wrist – to disclose a pair of tattooed letters in the shaven armpit: DD

'Mean anything to you?' she asked.

Cobb shook his head. 'Memento of some youthful folly, perhaps,' he essayed. 'It's by no means a new tattoo. Quite

94

old, in fact. Faded to a pale blue. Of no interest pathologically. I'll put it in the report, though. And you could perhaps raise the point with her sister when you see her.'

Leaving the mortuary assistants to tidy up the body and clear away, they parted company to shower and dress. Cobb was due at Plymouth that afternoon, and he reminded her to call in and see Nancy Chambers' sister.

The waiting room at the Cornwall and St Costello District General Hospital was furnished on the same lavish scale as the rest of the establishment, which had been conceived and built during the term of office of a former administration with an eye to vote catching – a misplaced hope as it turned out.

There was a twenty-four-hour self-service canteen attached, seating for a couple of hundred visitors and staff below the rank of Sister, bookshop and news stand, confectioner's kiosk – but no sale of tobacco.

Meg Chambers was waiting for her at a table near the entrance. She got to her feet when Tina came in. This came as no surprise to the latter, who had by now become accustomed to instant recognition – the price of being a celebrity. She herself would have picked out the other quite easily from her resemblance to dead Nancy.

Three paces into the room, approaching the other woman, Tina was stopped in her tracks by the almost tangible shock wave of hostility issuing from Meg Chambers' whole demeanour: her pursed mouth, eyes narrowed with malevolence, head thrust forward in a posture of aggression, her very stance.

'Um, good morning, Miss Chambers,' said Tina, extending her hand. 'I'm Tina May.'

'Aye – that's as may be,' responded the other enigmatically, and declined the proffered hand.

Remembering that the woman was recently bereaved, and mindful of Cobb's warning, Tina determined to make plenty of allowance for Meg Chambers' behaviour. 'Shall we sit down?' she said mildly.

Scowling, her companion did so, and Tina took stock of her. As her sister had described, Meg was in her forties – but aping the dress and appearance of a woman ten or fifteen years her junior, with hair frizzed and bleached blonde; wearing jeans, trainers, and a T-shirt with the legend: 'Dig Me'.

'All I want to know from you,' she said, eyeing Tina narrowly, 'is what our Nancy was like before she was killed. What she said, and all that.'

And, damn you – thought Tina – that is exactly what you *will* get. *And* you'll get a strictly edited version for your rudeness. . . .

'Nancy was quite cheerful,' she said. 'We hadn't met before, but we got on quite well. She appeared to me to be very competent and knowledgeable about cars, and a good driver. . . .'

'She was always mechanically minded,' interposed the other. 'Cars, motorbikes and such. Ever since she was a girl.' And her uncompromising features softened for the first time.

Tina, seizing upon the thaw, leapt in with an idea that had come to her mind: 'Did she service her own car – the taxi?' she asked.

The sullen suspiciousness closed in again upon her companion's attitude. 'That's just what the police asked me,' she replied. 'Yes, she did – and what of it?'

'Just a thought,' said Tina. (So Meg had not been told about the tampering with the wheel. The police might have informed me that they were keeping it dark!)

'So what else did you talk about?' demanded the woman, who had quite reverted to her narrow-eyed malevolence. 'Not just about motorcars – don't give me that!'

'In fact, we didn't talk about cars at all,' said Tina. 'She asked me if I was enjoying my holiday at Clifftop. I said yes – apart from the upset over Mrs Wakeley's death. And then she. . . .'

'And then she – *what?*' The interjection came as quick as a flash, and Tina, who had decided to fudge this particular issue with the overexcited woman, then changed her mind:

'Your sister introduced the topic of – the coven,' she said. 'And how she disapproved of Mrs Wakeley for being part of it.'

Meg Chambers exhaled a long, slow breath: one might have thought that this admission was what she had been waiting for.

'Did she bring *my* name into it?'

The question was not to be evaded; nor did Tina attempt to do so: 'Yes, she did.'

'I expect the two of you had a right old time pulling me to pieces,' cried the other.

'I made no comment,' responded Tina coldly. 'Your sister, as I recall, bent herself over backwards to make excuses for you.'

'Now, wasn't that kind of her?' sneered Meg Chambers.

'It was very typically – sisterly,' said Tina.

They sat in silence for a full half-minute, and Tina was just about to make her excuses and leave when her companion sprang a surprise question on her.

'You're a pal of that Doctor Heymans feller, aren't you?'

'He's a friend of mine – yes,' said Tina guardedly. 'Why?'

'*Another one of 'em!*'

The declaration was delivered in a near-shout; even people half-way down the room turned to stare.

'What *do* you mean?' demanded Tina.

'He killed – the Master!' Tina was left in no doubt about the status of the person to whom she referred: it was Master with a capital M! 'It was thanks to his mumbo-jumbo that Ellis Duke went and drowned himself. That Heymans feller did it with his spells, just as surely as if he'd thrown him into the sea and held him under!'

Tina was by this time on her feet, and feeling herself go red with anger and disgust. 'You stupid creature!' she said in even tones, summoning all the self-control she possessed. 'No,

97

I withdraw that – you've suffered a sad loss and your mind's disturbed. I suggest you go home, take a couple of aspirins and lie down.' She turned to go.

Meg Chambers had by no means finished with her. In full view – and hearing – of the assembled company, she pointed a finger at Tina and denounced:

'You're both in it together – you and that Heymans feller! He worked his spells on the Master till that wonderful man took the only way out of his misery.

'And now *you've* come here!

'First Mrs Wakeley dies – and now my sister! . . .

'Who's next on your list – *witch!*'

'I don't say she's certifiable. I wouldn't put it any higher than the antics of an overwrought neurotic – but it must have been most unpleasant for you, Tina.'

The police had driven her back to the cottage. On an impulse, she phoned Dermot Heymans as soon as she got in and told him about her humiliating encounter with Meg Chambers.

'It was, Dermot,' she replied. 'What do you suggest I do? To be honest, my inclination is to pack up right away, shake the dust of Trepoll Haven from my boots, and go home. My so-called retreat's been about as restful as putting up a tent in the middle of the M1 motorway!'

Heymans laughed. 'Nevertheless, it's doing you good – Trepoll Haven's benefiting you, and no mistake!'

'Dermot, how can you say such a thing?' She was almost amused, despite herself. 'It isn't funny to be publicly branded as a witch!'

'I'm quite serious,' he said. And she could almost see his mobile countenance switch from comedy to tragedy. 'The fact that you are responding positively and aggressively to your situation tells me that the cure is beginning to work. You are no longer the tragic, yet brilliant young pathologist it's just too bad about – you're reverting to hard-nosed, no-

nonsense Doctor Tina. What's more, I'll lay odds of ten to one that you'll stay in Trepoll and straighten out the situation there – neurotic Meg Chambers and all!'

Tina laughed. 'Oh, Dermot, you are a cure. You've made me feel better already. But, since you're determined that I shall stay, you must give me the lowdown on Ellis Duke's suicide, since the indications are that it may still be playing an important part in the happenings down here. I take it that what that silly woman was pleased to call your spells and mumbo-jumbo didn't in the end drive Duke to make an end of himself?'

'Only by default,' replied Heymans. 'His psychosis apart, by the time Duke came to me, there was no way back for him. The complication of drugs, debauchery, drink, and an unshakable conviction of his own divinity – yes, I said divinity – determined his inevitable end when none of the stimulants helped him any more, and his belief in personal divinity had to be put to the ultimate test.'

'What test was that?' asked Tina.

'Didn't I tell you before?' He sounded surprised. 'Duke spoke of it to me many times. It was inevitable that he would try to prove it to us all sooner or later.'

'Prove what?'

'That he could walk on water.'

Determined upon a quiet afternoon and evening, with a little reading, a minimum of radio, and an early night for once, she showered and washed her hair.

Not entirely to her surprise, Heymans had displayed no great interest in either of the two deaths – dismissing them, no doubt, as being of no psychological import. Nor, oddly, had he reacted strongly to her account of the midnight orgy on the beach; he opined that, yes, it might well have comprised the leftovers of Duke's coven, but the village copper was right: there was an awful lot of that sort of thing going on among teenagers.

And still – for reasons she was unable to analyse – she had said nothing to him about the severed head.

The ambition for a quiet afternoon was easily achieved with no phone calls or visitors; she read in the garden, baked one of her favourite cakes, listened in to her favourite literary discussion-cum-quiz, even dozed off for half an hour in the sunshine.

In the cool of the early evening she had an impulse to exercise. Taking her stout walking stick she went down the staircase to the beach and, avoiding the west (memories of the midnight orgy!), set off towards the east and the haven. The tide was well out, allowing her to walk actually round the seaward side of the breakwater and enter the tiny harbour from the business end. There the small fishing boats were lying forlornly in a couple of inches of water, with a few young children splashing around them, while the fisher-folk worked on their nets on the shingle, or sat in groups, smoking and gossiping as the long shadows closed over the narrow enclave and the seabirds whirled, screeching, overhead.

A few pairs of eyes were turned to see the tall, striking-looking woman in a shabby mack and headscarf, but this disguise, coupled with dark glasses (an ensemble invented by the British Royals and taken up by celebrities the world over), ensured her anonymity.

Or – almost. . . .

She had climbed up the sloping slipway from the shingle, and joined the throng of tourists and holidaymakers who moved up and down that part of the village street skirting the foreshore, and had turned homewards, when she saw a half-familiar face coming straight towards her along the pavement. A moment's search of memory placed the other as PC Tuttle's garrulous neighbour Mrs Slyte – and it was clear, from the woman's sudden attention, that she had penetrated her camouflage. Tina assembled a nod, a smile and a 'good evening' in readiness.

She gave a nod, the smile died in a rictus grin, and the greeting was stillborn – as with a very pointed avoidance of her eye, Mrs Slyte turned abruptly and darted up a narrow entry between two houses fronting the street. When Tina came abreast of the entry, she paused and gazed up there, to see the woman's figure scurrying like a frightened mouse – almost running away from her!

Puzzled, rather disturbed, and not one wit amused by the curious non-encounter, Tina shook her head and, crossing the street, made for W. Penlee – General Store, with the intention of picking up a few provisions and a picture postcard or two for her scrapbook. Half-way there, she distinctly saw Mr Penlee eyeing her through the glass doorway – though not very clearly, because the inside of the panel was hung with magazines, posters, notices and the like. There was also a quite prominent notice hung on a piece of string announcing that the shop was OPEN.

By the time Tina had negotiated the kerb and the half-dozen paces remaining, the notice had been turned round to read: CLOSED.

As she stood there for a moment or so, irresolute, the lights inside the shop were switched off, and a door banged beyond.

Underneath the CLOSED notice was another, announcing that the shop was open weekdays in the season from 9 a.m. to 7 p.m.

By her watch, the time was shy of seven by a quarter of an hour and more.

She ate her supper of home-made lasagne to a concert of Vivaldi on the local radio. This was followed by a news programme in which the lead item concerned the death of Nancy Chambers on the Trepoll–St Costello road the previous day. The smash had already been announced several times and described as an accident. Significantly, it had now taken the form of a police statement: the word 'accident' was omitted, and 'tragic occurrence' substituted, and 'police inquiries into the cause of the crash are continuing'. Tina wondered wryly what Meg Chambers was making of that.

She had cleared away and was washing up in the kitchen sink when there came a double knock-knock on the front door. Instantly, she froze. That door, like everything else in the cottage, doors and windows both, was securely fastened by every means provided. But it was dusk. In view of the disturbing happenings since her arrival, she felt terribly vulnerable, marooned as she was up on the heights above the village, and all alone.

The knock was not repeated. She waited a few moments longer and then, taking up the walking stick, she crossed the living room and went to see who it was – if he or she still remained.

There was a very sensible arrangement of a thick woollen curtain acting as a draught-excluder hanging from above the door to floor level, which had to be drawn aside before the door could be opened.

Tina was looking up when she drew the curtain along its rail, so she did not see the thing that was coiled up on the floor immediately underneath the letterbox; indeed, she saw and heard nothing till after her slippered foot brushed up against something that moved, and she immediately suffered an agonizing bite in her bare ankle.

She cried out. Dropped the stick in her shock. Reached down to touch the hurt ankle – and saw the neat coils gathered close by her foot, the tiny, diamond-shaped head with the V-marking on the flattened skull, the pattern of dark diamonds extending from neck to tail, the eyes like drowned seed pearls, the flickering tongue.

It was a sizeable adder, and it had come – someone had put it – through the letter box! *For her!*

Fury informed Tina's actions, then. No fear. She picked up the stick, and when the creature glided away for cover, she struck at it, so that it writhed, showing its pale underbelly among the tangled coils.

'Damn you – damn you – damn you!' she shouted, lashing

at the snake again and again, knowing no fear – only outrage.

She kept hitting till the writhing had ceased, and then, uncaring of the cool, dry touch of the reptilian skin – which she had never dreamed willingly to touch, would have suffered almost anything than touch – she gathered up the slack coils, wrenched open a window, and threw the dead snake out into the night.

'*Take it – it's yours!*' she shouted to anyone who was out there.

Brave words! – but there remained the bite: two small punctures just above the ankle bone of the left leg. The pain was intense and the wound had already taken on a dark purple discoloration. Mindful of her training in first aid, she rigged a tourniquet out of a dishcloth and a dessert spoon, tightening it till she reckoned that the circulation of blood was reduced to a minimum. She then went to the phone.

Tom Cobb's number rang out unanswered, but then she remembered that he had gone to Plymouth. One hand on the tourniquet, she dug out Heymans' list of useful local people and found the name and number of the local General Practitioner. It was not encouraging:

Dr Lucius Strang – Fossilized somewhere around 1920. Couldn't
(Tel. T.H. 031)   diagnose a common cold. Consult only in an
                   emergency – otherwise call Dr Cobb (q.v.)

Doctor Strang sounded like Heymans' word-picture: a quavering old man's voice and an air of bewilderment.

'Adder bite, you say?'

'That's right, I've just been bitten in the ankle.'

'You sure it was an adder? Not confusing it with a grass snake? You sound like a city person, and city people aren't well versed in the fauna of the countryside. A grass snake, you see, is quite harml. . . .'

'It was an adder!' snapped Tina. 'I killed it. Now I've put on a tourniquet, and I'd be grateful if you'd come over and inject the requisite antivenin, please.'

103

'Antivenin, is it? Oh, you are very well informed.' This was followed by a cackle of old man's laughter. 'I'll be right over. Sit quietly till I arrive. Keep calm and don't exert yourself.'

'Hey!' cried Tina. 'Don't you want to know my address?'

'Address? Oh! Yes, of *course* I want your address, my dear young lady. How else shall I find you?'

She told him – and with a numb feeling of despair.

Dr Lucius Strang looked and talked like a barnstorming actor-manager of the old school, with a white mane of hair worn long in the neck, commanding eyes of washed-out blue, a Roman profile. Masked by the quavering, the voice carried the rich timbre of a well-played old cello. The name of Tina May meant nothing to him. His manners were beautiful.

'What we have here, my dear young lady,' he said, taking a phial of straw-coloured liquid from his battered black bag, together with a hypodermic, 'is the specific antivenin for *Vipera berus*, the common European adder. It is an indispensable item in the armoury of the West Country physician, since the adder is indigenous to this area.' He filled the hypodermic, emitted the air, and advanced the point towards Tina. 'The antivenin is obtained by submitting horses to repeated sub-lethal doses of venom till the animal produces serum which possesses specific immunity. A remarkably ingenious notion you may think, young lady. But a helluva way to treat a noble animal like a horse, eh?' After apologizing for what he called his 'lapse into verbal vulgarity', the old man chuckled. He then injected Tina with what she was relieved to discern as devastating expertise.

'How big was the reptile?' he asked, sitting back and carefully replacing the instrument in his bag. 'I should like to see it, if still available.'

'I picked it up and chucked it out of the window when I'd killed it,' said Tina.

'Did you now?' The rheumy eyes were regarding her

thoughtfully. 'Very much the modern young lady, eh? No shrinking violet, you. Frightened of nothing.'

'Frankly, snakes used to scare the hell out of me,' said Tina. 'But not any longer. Whoever put that adder through my letter box all inadvertently did me a good turn. I'm cured of a snake phobia that's haunted me since childhood.'

The old physician let quite a while go by before he responded. This he did in the same calm, unruffled voice as ever: 'Did I hear aright, young lady? Did you say someone deliberately put. . . .' He sketched the remainder of his question by gesturing towards the front door with an elegantly expressive hand.

'Yes,' said Tina. 'And not in a spirit of fun.'

'Did you say fun? Indeed not. For though the human death rate from the bite of *Vipera berus* is negligible, it will give you an exceedingly unpleasant twenty-four hours, young lady.

'Have you any idea who might have been the donor of this ill-conceived gift?' he asked.

'No,' said Tina, and then, entirely upon an impulse, which may have been inspired by a sudden liking that she had taken to this sedate old party, she added: 'Do *you* have any idea, Doctor?'

'Do I – did you say do *I?*' he gave her a glance that was part-mischievous, part-quizzical, and all shrewdness. 'Well, now. I might – but I would have to give it some thought. By the by, are you by chance well acquainted with Doctor Heymans, the owner of this establishment?'

'He's a friend of mine,' said Tina.

'Ah – then I must keep a guard on my tongue,' said the old man with a twinkle of his fugitive blue eye. 'You see, I once badly blotted my copybook with the egregious Heymans when I opined that not only was Freudian psychiatry a load of old rope, but that time would manifestly show it to be so. Consequently, we are no longer – as my old nanny used to say – "on speakers".'

He rose to leave. 'I will give some thought to your question,' he said. 'Meantime, my only suggestion – and it is

105

based on the fact that Doctor Heymans is by no means popular in the village – is that, because of your relationship with Heymans, some of the animosity felt towards him may have rubbed off on to you. But I will put my mind to your question and let you know.

'By the way,' he added, pausing at the door, 'do you have an occupation, young lady, or are you what used to be described as: "Of Independent Means"?'

Tina smiled. It was so refreshing to be unrecognized for once, and merely a 'young lady'. 'I'm a pathologist,' she said.

'Ah!' He expressed slight surprise. 'Well, I should like you to take a couple of aspirin and go to bed. Plenty of rest and quiet. Telephone me tomorrow if you are in discomfort.'

'Thank you, Doctor,' said Tina meekly.

'I predict a swift recovery for you,' he declared. 'But then, you have no doubt already discerned that from the stars – after the arcane fashion of your calling. Good night.'

He left Tina with a question teetering on her lips. It was not till later that she reasoned out the answer to his curious declaration.

The old man, who had demonstrated that he was a bit deaf, must have misheard 'pathologist' as 'astrologist' – presumably his own archaic term for 'astrologer'.

Madame Tina – What the Stars Foretell!

She laughed – and it turned to a yelp of pain, as her snake-bitten ankle gave an agonizing throb.

Seven

Tina slept that night, but intermittently, and bedevilled with a high temperature, nausea and depression. As so often happens in the hour or so before dawn when the soul is most easily wrenched from its earthly tabernacle, she drifted into a peaceful slumber, from which she woke when the sun came in through the uncurtained window and bathed her in its warm light. She sat up and felt surprisingly better, and when she took off the light bandage which Doctor Strang had given her, she found that the angry discoloration had gone from the bite, and that the two tiny punctures were showing signs of healing up nicely.

'So – hooray for the horses,' said Tina.

She limped downstairs, picking up a small pile of mail (first making sure that no unwanted benefactions accompanied it), but found there to be neither newspaper nor milk. She next made herself comfortable on a wicker armchair in the kitchen with her injured leg propped up on a stool, and sipped at a mug of instant coffee while she read her letters.

The first was from Maggie, posted the previous day, Tuesday:

Dear Tina,

What an awful way to start your 'retreat'. Everyone who knows you is saying how disgusting the *Sunday Courier* article struck them; how snide, underhand, obviously malicious, etc.

People have been ringing to get your address and phone number in Cornwall, but I have dutifully refused to give either – even in the case of the TV people (hope I did right here!). Your producer Simon Elles rang most insistently, but finally settled for my forwarding a letter to you myself. Would you believe? – it was round here by hand within a quarter of an hour! (Herewith enclosed.)

Another caller was Detective Sgt Vance, who rang to ask me to pass on to you the news that the man Holmes was found to have pawned his common-law wife's pieces of jewellery the day after she died of the stab wound, and they have arrested him on the strength of it. (The point was that Holmes had strenuously denied having any knowledge of the jewellery. I suppose the police trapped the poor wretch with their tricksy-wicksy questioning.)

On the home front, no news of Jock. I expect you're right, and we shan't see anything of him till his 'partner' has run off with all the money. The progress of Jock Junior continues apace. I won't bore you with the details, but I really am getting quite broody about the whole process. Best and happiest time I've ever had!

Do look after yourself. .

Love,

    Maggie

The accompanying envelope was of a most disconcertingly thick and expensive hand-made paper, emblazoned on the flap with the arms of the TV company. The enclosed single sheet of writing paper was similarly impressive. Not so the message it contained; it was both short and disturbingly equivocal:

Dear Tina,

Such secrecy! Garbo at her most withdrawn was never so hard to contact as yourself. However, Mohammed must perforce go to the mountain. . . .

Greatly hope that the rest is doing you good in your corner of darkest Cornwall. All our thoughts are with you, darling.

You will be cheered to hear that the next series of *The Pathologist* is to be put back till after the New Year. This is to allow plenty of time to do a little rethinking on such matters as publicity, presentation, and maybe a tightening up of the programmes at the 'drawing board stage' but still to be shot.

With the useful time in hand, we might also consider revamping some of those already in the can.

So you see, Tina, we still have you and *The Pathologist* very much in mind.

Everyone sends love.

Yours ever,
    Simon

Tina thought she saw it all very clearly: the scurrilous *Sunday Courier* piece had set the cat amongst the pigeons at TV House: beginning with the board of directors, forever sensitive as any hypocritical whore to attacks upon their corporate virtue; and down to Simon Elles himself, who had been the butt of sly digs from the gutter press ever since he left his wife to go and keep house with the show's director Gerry Hackett-Bryce. But, most of all, the image of the cool, magisterial Doctor Tina May had been shockingly dented by the article. She whom a critic had dubbed 'that latter-day Portia, that Diana chaste and fair, that Aphrodite of Hippocrates': such extravagant veneration does not long survive the vision of a shrill, neurotic female run amok, under psychiatric treatment and living it up in a 'luxury villa' in Cornwall.

To her, it was all as clear as a bell: the powers that be had left their options open either to kill *The Pathologist*, or to play a waiting game till after the New Year and then see what the polls had to say about the show's – and the star's – standing with the viewing public.

It was all bitterly depressing. She laid Elles' letter aside with a very clear vision of herself set right back where she had been two years previously: gone her living-in secretary, the modest luxuries of occasional weekends in Paris, winter sporting in Gstaad, being on good terms with one's bank manager and unfearful of the bills that dropped upon the mat; most of all her own personal yardstick of affluence: choosing what one wanted most of all from a restaurant menu without having to check up on the price. She supposed that she would settle down again to being a hard-working, modestly-paid pathologist – but the reversion might be a bit painful at first.

The phone rang. She hopped on one leg to answer it.

'Doctor Strang here. Ha–ha, my dear young lady, you have been teasing me. You have been "having me on" – as my dear old mother used to say.'

'I – I'm afraid I don't understand,' began Tina, thinking as she said so that she understood only too well.

'Ha! My housekeeper, Mrs Penhallow, has told me who you really are, my dear Doctor Tina May. She tells me that you are what I believe is known as a "celebrity" on the wireless-television. Correct?'

'Correct,' she replied, amused.

'And how are we this morning?'

'Much better, thanks to you – and to those poor horses.'

'Ah. Good. Then I will call and see you later on this morning, after I have called upon Wakeley, poor old fellow.'

'The vicar – how is he?' asked Tina, mindful of her resolve to call upon the tragic widower.

'Very poorly, I'm afraid,' said Strang. 'But more of that when we meet. Ah – and also. . . .'

'Yes, Doctor Strang?'

'Also, dear young lady, I have been searching my mind, and am now able to throw some light upon the identity of your late visitor – ah – Beware the Greeks bearing gifts.'

'I shall look forward to that,' said Tina. And put down the phone.

So I shall, she thought. Let our profession stick together, as laymen popularly suppose, through thick and thin, right and wrong. She sensed she had an ally in old Strang like the one she had in Tom Cobb. With neither of them, surely, was there any need to withhold confidences.

Speaking of Cobb reminded her of the small puzzle they had uncovered during the post mortem on Nancy Chambers: because of that humiliating scene with the dead woman's sister, she had never got around to asking Meg about the DD rune under Nancy's armpit. . . .

110

Her proximity to the phone prompted her to ring the village store to find what had happened to the usual early morning delivery.

This she did. . . .

'General stores, Trepoll.'

'Mr Penlee, this is Doctor May. I don't seem to have had my milk and newspaper.'

'The dairy van hasn't been 'smorning,' came the smug reply.

'When are you expecting it?'

'Mebbe won't come now.' With a note of satisfaction.

'Well, I wonder if the boy could bring me up a tin of condensed milk, or some powdered milk, when he brings the newspaper?'

'Got no delivery boy this morning.' There was no mistaking the triumph.

'Oh. Well, can't someone come up? I'm incapacitated?'

'There's only me in the shop.' Game, set and match – he supposed.

Tina had a very clear image, in her mind's eye, of Penlee's tight, buttoned-up face all full of malice when he had deliberately locked his shop door on her the previous evening; now he must be grinning.

She saw red. 'Then why don't you shut up shop and do the delivery yourself?' she snapped.

'Now see here,' he began, affronted, 'I won't be talked to like. . . .'

She hung up on him and felt better.

He was all actor-manager this morning: a dramatic cloak thrown back over one shoulder of a shiny black suit, a curly-brimmed black felt hat worn jauntily on one side of his white-maned head.

'Ha, you've had a fine jest with me, my dear young lady,' he said. 'Telling me you were an astrologist, indeed.' He beamed fondly at her.

111

Tina let it pass. 'I'm sorry,' she said.

'And how are you now?'

'Much better still. I just feel as if I'm in the last day of a dose of flu.'

'That's normal. Let me have a look at it.'

She stretched out her leg and he stooped beside her chair and looked closely at the wound, after affixing a pince-nez that hung on a black moiré ribbon round his neck.

'Mmm. No more trouble there than you'd have had from a couple of bad bee stings. Mark you, I am always inclined to treat the bite of *Vipera berus* with the correct degree of gravity, particularly when small children or the aged and infirm are involved.' He glanced sharply up at her. 'Speaking of age and decrepitude, you were asking about old Wakeley. You have a particular interest in his case, so my housekeeper informs me.'

'I was called to the holiday camp when his wife was found drowned in the pool there,' replied Tina. 'And I did a preliminary p.m.'

'Ah, yes. I was not sent for, of course. I should tell you, my dear doctor – and speaking as one to another – my medical talents are no longer very highly regarded in Trepoll Haven.' He delivered the declaration quite cheerfully, and without a hint of resentment or self-pity.

'If anyone has any doubts about *your* medical expertise, let them say as much in my hearing!' said Tina.

'You are kind,' said the old man. 'However, concerning the Honourable Reverend Arthur Wakeley – to give him his full styling – and, by the way, my dear Doctor, if you have the makings of a pot of tea, I will do the honours for us both. . . .'

Tina gestured. 'Sure. Tea's in that tin. Remainder of yesterday's milk in the fridge. You were saying? . . .'

Strang filled the electric kettle and switched it on. 'His wife's death has cut the ground from beneath Arthur's feet,' he said, 'not that his feet were ever placed very firmly on the ground to begin with. You met the Honourable Mrs Wakeley when alive?' He glanced sidelong at her, lifting down the tea tin.

'Briefly. Once. The afternoon before her death.'

112

'How did she strike you?'

'Well, obviously much younger than her husband. Vivacious. More sparklingly vital than anyone I've ever met, I think. Almost too – it sounds a very odd thing to say, I know – but almost *too* scintillating. Like – like some shooting star, a dazzling comet, that's doomed to burn itself out at its very brightest.'

The old man paused in the act of switching off the boiling kettle. 'How very prescient of you,' he said, 'or are you perhaps speaking from the benefit of hindsight?'

'No – I had that feeling about her right away.'

'A faultless appreciation.' He scaled the teapot. 'Given her situation, I would say that Glenda Wakeley was pre-ordained for an early death – a relatively early death, to be exact.' Again, his eye was cocked towards her. 'In your examination, did you find anything to suggest – say – suicide?'

Tina saw the Rubicon before her and stepped boldly across it. 'In the opinion of Doctor Cobb and myself, she was murdered!' she said.

If Strang was surprised – astounded – shocked – by her declaration, he did not show it; with steady hands, he poured the contents of the re-boiled kettle on to the tea in the bottom of the scalded pot.

'Excellent young fellow, that Doctor Cobb,' he opined. 'Thought so from the first when he came here. Would have offered him a partnership – Strang and Cobb – but it seemed presumptuous.

'You have good evidence – forensic evidence – to support your contention?' he asked.

'No,' said Tina. 'Given a possible culprit and a motive, one might have a starting point, though.

'By the way, Doctor,' she added. 'Can you tell me anything about the coven which used to operate – probably still operates actively – in Trepoll Haven?'

He shook his head. 'I cannot,' he said. 'One had heard mutterings, but I am not *au fait* with such activities, and they could be taking place without my scarcely being aware.

113

Certainly, as I understand, the late Ellis Duke was concerned in such things – his skilful but appalling murals in this place bear evidence – but whether the influence still continues, I wouldn't know, and no one would think to tell me. No one tells me anything.

'Sugar? No?'

'I sidetracked you,' said Tina. 'You were telling me about the vicar and his wife, and his reaction to her – death.'

'Total collapse!' said Strang. 'I have never seen anyone deteriorate so completely, so swiftly. You implied that you have met him? . . .'

'Once,' said Tina. 'Again, it was on the day before she was killed. The impression I got – very strongly – was that of a frightened man. Yet, despite that, he was most concerned about my well-being and invited me to go to him for help if I was in any need. I thought it was possibly just the cleric in him mouthing the usual platitudes – but I'm not so sure.'

'Speaking as a lifelong atheist of the old Fabian school, I'd normally be inclined to think it was a platitude,' said Lucius Strang, 'but I would make an exception in the case of Arthur Wakeley. He is essentially a *good* man.'

'Much put upon, would you say?' asked Tina, watching the other's reaction over the rim of her teacup.

'By the flighty wife?' Strang raised an eyebrow and grinned knowingly. 'I have no doubt on that score. Not to speak ill of the dead, but la Glenda was widely regarded as the Messalina of South Cornwall. With branches all over the country, I don't doubt. Oh, yes, poor old Arthur had ample opportunities to practise his Christian charity, forbearance and forgiveness, I don't doubt.'

'Mmmm,' mused Tina. 'Well, I think that, harking back to what we were saying a few minutes ago, about evidence in support of Glenda having been murdered, I would say that a lover – a current lover – would be a prime suspect, given the slight forensic evidence we unearthed.'

She waited a moment, and added: 'Do you have anyone in mind for the role, Doctor Strang?'

114

He drained his teacup and reached to pour himself another ill. 'Ah, you search me out very closely, my dear young lady,' ie said. 'I shall have to give that some thought. Yes, that will all for some very careful sifting of impressions.'

(He knows, she thought. He's a mine of gossip of the *selective* ind one would associate with an old gentleman who kept his yes and ears open, but didn't get around much – and he could name a name right here and now.)

'I must go,' said Strang, finishing his second cup of tea in wift order. 'Delighted at your excellent recovery from the bite, and much elevated by our discourse. You must come and have tea with me quite soon, if you can bear to endure the truly Dickensian squalor in which I exist.'

'I'm sure you live like a prince,' said Tina. And, as he went towards the door: 'By the way, you were going to think it over and tell me who, in your opinion, put the snake through my letter box.'

He had almost reached the front door, and she was limping after him with the aid of the walking stick, before he replied: 'I have given it some thought, Doctor,' he said. 'And I'm half-way to convincing myself that I could name a name. However' – He turned to regard her, his hand on the door latch – 'However, it now occurs to me that the donor of your *Vipera berus* and Glenda Wakeley's last lover could very well be one and the same person. In view of the grave implications of that possibility, I should like to sleep on it before I commit myself.

'Good day. my dear young lady.'

She watched his old car going down the lane: it had the movements of the chronically infirm: careful, hesitant, fearful of being hurt or of missing its step in the ruts and runnels. And she thought of how Strang's claim to be completely in the dark about the Trepoll Haven coven did not square with the fact of his being a mine of gossip about almost everything else one touched upon.

But he also brewed a very good pot of tea.

*

115

Detective Superintendent Derek Arkwright's oldest friend a Scotland Yard, his former chief and mentor whom th younger man had long since overtaken on the promotion ladder with no loss to their mutual esteem, was retiring at the end of the week and Arkwright was taking him out to lunch that day at his – the latter's — favourite restaurant. He had just about finished with making the table booking when hi assistant tapped on the door and came in.

'All right, Oscar. Table for two at one. I know I shoul have rung earlier, but you'll fit us in okay. You'd better What's that – police brutality? You'll know all about polic brutality if that table's not forthcoming. See you, Oscar.

'What is it, Turner?'

Detective Sergeant Turner's sharp-eyed gaze focused or his chief. It was a habit of his – to hold his listener's gaze in thrall when he spoke, as if seeking confirmation for his every turn of phrase, each line of argument. Arkwright had found i disconcerting in the early days of their relationship, but had come round to the belief that it was partly due to a short sightedness which the other concealed from vanity, insecurity a sense of inferiority – or all three.

'I haven't managed to get a lot of real hard info on our man, sir,' announced Turner.

'I think we'd be presumptuous to refer to him as "our man",' replied Arkwright. 'He's a long shot, to say the least Do go on.'

Not one bit put out, Turner referred to a sheaf of notes he carried.

'Born Cardiff,' he said. 'Background obscure, save that his father was registered as "Unknown" and he took his mother's maiden name. Twice married and divorced. No police record. Resided in France for ten years prior to returning to England, where he worked for about a year as an art director for a film company that went bust.'

'Photographs?'

'Only a couple, sir.' Turner slid two prints across Arkwright's desk and the other examined a head and

houlders profile of a heavily bearded man in a flat cap, and
nother of the same character – a rather muzzy outdoor
snapshot of him leaning against the balustrade of a bridge.

'The beard's a disappointment,' said Arkwright. 'He was
clean-shaven when he comes into our story. I doubt if anyone
would recognize him from this.'

'Agreed, sir,' was Turner's rueful reply. 'Particularly
Doctor May.'

'As you say – particularly Doctor May. Any medical
records?'

'None I can trace, sir. So far as his time in France is
concerned. I'm in contact with the Sûreté, and they're
following up every line.'

'What did he do in France?' asked Arkwright.

'Art direction. The movies. Theatre – opera and ballet.
Made a useful name for himself, but kept a low profile. No
fresh marital ventures recorded. After ten years, he decamped
back to England leaving no stir behind him. Next thing, he
turns up in Trepoll Haven as a tenant of Doctor Heymans,
who also treated him for a psychosis. You have a copy of
Heymans' case notes on file, sir.'

'Yes,' said Arkwright, 'and they don't tell me a lot.' He sat
back in his chair and regarded his assistant with the kind of
probing look that the other invariably employed on him.
'And it's your belief, Turner, that this man is the subject of
Tina May's severed head.'

'Duke is the best option we have, sir,' responded Turner. 'If
I may go over the reasons again. One – knowing Doctor May,
there's no doubt that when she claims to have made brief
contact with the severed head of an adult male unknown to
her, she did just that. Two – among missing persons reported,
we've been able to account for every adult male within a fifty-
mile radius of Trepoll Haven – save one.'

'Ellis Duke,' supplied Arkwright. 'Missing, believed
drowned, eight months ago.'

'Whose severed head turns up in his last place of abode –
having been deep frozen for that specific period.'

117

'An imaginative hypothesis, Turner,' said his chief, 'and well up to your usual standard. But it doesn't get us much further unless Doctor May can make a positive identification from the photos, which – considering that she described the severed head in her statement as being clean-shaven – I doubt if she'll be able. But send her the prints.'

'Through the local constabulary?' asked Turner.

'No, no. Exercise a bit of discretion – the Yard hasn't been called in. Not yet.

'Send the pictures direct to Doctor May. Ask her to ring me if she comes up with a positive identification – which I doubt.'

Later that day Tina had a ring from Tom Cobb:

'Old Strang called to see me and told me about your snake bite,' he said. 'What a frightful thing to happen. Are you okay?'

'Right as rain,' she replied. 'Combination of your local brew of antivenin, or else the adder was having a menopause, or maybe it's my excellent constitution, but all I have now is a soreness and slight lameness. Nice of you to call.'

'Look,' said Cobb, 'I'm really ringing to ask if you'd like an afternoon out tomorrow. According to the weather boys, this marvellous summer's going to go out with a bang within the next thirty-six hours, so one might as well make the most of it. I thought of taking a picnic tea and driving along to Dorwel Head. How does that grab you?'

'That would be lovely.'

'See you then. About three. Don't worry about the eats. Mother's making us up a hamper and she's the best in the business.'

'Looking forward to it, Tom.'

And Tina decided that she really was looking forward to a change of scenery – to get away from the growingly claustrophobic, not to say menacing, atmosphere of Trepoll Haven. And in such engaging company.

*

Tina had seen, and admired, Dorwell Head from afar. Crouching like some predatory beast into the waste of the Atlantic, it was the far headland that bounded the wide bay to the west of Trepoll Haven, and the venue of the lighthouse that sent its pencil beam sweeping over the night seas. On a clear day it looked only a hop, skip and a jump from Trepoll; by road along darkest Cornwall's tortuous, winding, drystone-walled lanes, it was an hour and a half's drive that was not made easier by the antics of Tom Cobb's fellow knights of the road. As he pointed out, the tourists – mostly town-dwellers – were unused to the West Country convention of negotiating what were substantially one-way lanes with an eye on the occasional passing-places conveniently cut into the verges every two or three hundred yards, to enable one to duck inside for a moment and let the other fellow through; with a tourist (Cornish folk call them 'emmets', which is duchy dialect for 'ants'), one is constantly brought vis-à-vis an arche-typical red-faced father of family with a car-load of bored, wail-ing offspring who has no intention of backing up to the passing-place that he did not happen to notice just before he came round the bend.

Presently, however, this via dolorosa had been negotiated and they arrived at the pleasant sweep of greensward dotted with Mediterranean pine that topped the high cliff of Dorwell Head, with its white-painted lighthouse poised like an exclamation mark at the far tip, overlooking the waves that seethed among the sharp rocks far below.

They picked out a quiet spot and put down the car rug and cushions.

'It's so beautiful – so peaceful,' said Tina.

'Thought you'd like it,' said Cobb. 'I often bring Mother here, and she says that the very sounds and the feel of the place describe the scenery to her as vividly as any pair of eyes could tell.'

Tina leaned back on one elbow, looked out to the east, to

119

the granite finger of Trepoll's breakwater half-way along the bay, and had the delicacy to allow a few moments to pass before she pursued the topic of the blind Mrs Cobb.

'I'm afraid I'm not very well up on the theatre,' she said 'but I gathered from the pictures in your waiting room that your mother must have been a professional?'

'Oh, yes,' said Cobb, 'she was reckoned to have quite considerable promise in her young days. She played many of the lesser Shakespearean roles, Shaw, Pinero – till she went blind.'

'What a tragedy – it must have affected her very deeply,' said Tina.

'Not as much as it might,' said Cobb. 'She had premonitions about blindness ever since childhood, and was in a sense prepared. Just as she was prepared for my father being killed in the war.'

'Second sight?'

'Something like that. I don't understand it. It isn't in our courses of medical study, is it, Tina? But there can't be a practising doctor who hasn't come up against this thing – call it second sight, prophecy, clairvoyance, or whatever.' He narrowed his deep brown eyes against the glare of the sun and looked out across the glassy sea towards a yacht that was trailing a herringbone wake close inshore. 'And Mother has it, that's for sure.'

'I'm a part-believer myself,' said Tina, 'though without very much concrete evidence. And I must say that, familiar with the common clay of death as I am, one isn't over-conscious of spirituality. Some say one becomes hardened to death as an end product. I don't think I am, not particularly.'

He looked down at her. 'Why did you go into forensic pathology, Tina?' he asked.

She smiled. 'That's pretty much a stock question for me,' she said, 'and I'll give you the stock answer which I've edited, fine-honed and clarified throughout the years.

'My early inclination was towards paediatrics, but the first time I saw a child die of meningitis – I sat and held her hand

120

hrough the night – I knew I didn't have what it takes. Then I met Johnny Kettle, who led me towards pathology and taught me all I know. And part of it was self-knowledge: I don't fear death, nor do dead bodies trouble me greatly; what I can't bear is the process of dying. As a fellow student of mine once remarked when, after going through much the same experience as myself, he went into dentistry after he'd qualified as a physician: "Folks don't die of teeth". My view's much the same: folks don't die of post-mortem examinations. End of story.'

'I, on the other hand, am a bit leery about what benevolent corruption does to human tissues,' countered Cobb. 'So before we avail ourselves of Mother's no doubt excellent comestibles, can I just talk to you for a few minutes about that severed head which landed on your doorstep?'

'That business,' said Tina, 'has rather died in the night. The local cops don't believe me, they think it's a product of my neurotic imagination. The only sympathetic hearing I've had so far – apart from yourself – has been from a detective friend of mine in Scotland Yard.'

'Ah, you're in touch with the Yard?'

'Under the Old Pals' Act – as well as in the line of business,' she replied. 'I worked with Derek Arkwright on my first big murder case.'*

'Does Arkwright have any theories as to who the dead man might be?'

'Derek put it this way,' she said. 'In his view, the identity can't be established till either the head turns up again – with or without the body – or I'm able to identify the victim from a photograph of some missing person or other. And I'm inclined to agree with that. What do you think?'

Cobb rubbed his jaw, deep in thought. Presently he said: 'I think, with local knowledge, I could take it a bit further than that. Now, I don't know the incidence of missing persons in south Cornwall, but I guess if one disregarded the missing

*In *No Escape* by Sarah Kemp

121

kids and missing females and concentrated on – what would
you say was the age of the man in question? . . .'

'Well-preserved forty-five to fifty,' she supplied.

'Concentrated on males in that age group, the number
would be pretty small.'

Tina thought she saw what was coming, and countered it
in advance: 'I'm pretty certain that the head had been deep
frozen, or at least refrigerated,' she said. 'That would widen
the search, since the tissues could have been in preservation –
well – almost indefinitely, of course. So how do you feel about
investigating all missing males of between forty-five and fifty
over the last – say – ten years? That would gross up your total
considerably.'

Cobb was not visibly put down by her argument; instead,
he became even more animated, more incisive.

'That very factor only strengthens my theory,' he declared.
'And I'll tell you what it is. . . .'

'I'm listening,' said Tina, intrigued.

'Who went missing, believed dead, but the body was never
found, in Trepoll eight months ago?'

'Oh!' exclaimed Tina. 'I suppose you're going to say. . . .'

'And his severed head turns up – quite fortuitously – in the
very cottage that he was residing in on the night he died.
Think about that!'

'Well, of course. . . .' she began.

'If you were to feed those facts into a computer,' persisted
Cobb, 'comparing them with the vital statistics on – as you
say – ten years' records of similarly missing persons – the
machine would come up with one answer – the strongest
mathematical possibility.'

'Ellis Duke,' said Tina.

'Well?' He stared at her, head on one side, looking absurdly
boyish and earnest.

'I can't fault your theory as regards possibility,' said Tina.
'Proving it might be difficult.'

'You could ask Scotland Yard to search out for photographs
of Duke.'

122

'Aren't there any in existence around the place – to your knowledge?' she asked.

He shook his head. 'Never come across any. But, then, I was no friend of Duke's. Scarcely knew him. But your detective Arkwright could get hold of such a thing – if there are any in existence. What do you think?'

Tina found herself caught up in the infection of his enthusiasm, and saw a situation where she could point a finger at a photo and swear on oath that this indeed was the man who had been reduced to a severed head; saw herself doing it – and the hell to that oaf Wainhouse, that sneering Tuttle and the rest.

'It's worth trying,' she said. 'I'll ring Derek Arkwright as soon as I get back to the cottage. How about that?'

'I certainly think it's worth doing,' said her companion. He nodded to himself and looked out towards the sea, and to the south-west, where the pellucid blueness of the sky had taken on an unhealthy yellow, and there were mares' tails up on high over the horizon.

'I reckon the weather boys were right, Tina,' he said, pointing. 'There's a storm on its way. I propose that we have tea while the going's still good.'

The going was still good – very good. The sun continued to beat down on their bit of Cornwall, the grasshoppers chirruped in the gorse bushes, the larks flew high, and the sea remained like a sheet of beaten blue steel; the yacht, which had passed the point of the headland below them when they sat down, was not making much headway before nearly-following light airs as it shaped course for distant Plymouth.

Mrs Cobb had indeed done them very well. There was tea and coffee in Thermos flasks, both hot and iced; sandwiches of foie gras, smoked salmon, ham and thinly sliced cucumber; home-made chocolate and Cornish cream cake that was enough to make a zealot throw away his calorie counter and surrender; Conference pears in syrup and more Cornish cream.

'I give up,' said Tina, later – very much later, balling up

her paper napkin and dropping it into the ravished picnic basket among the detritus.

'Me too,' grinned Cobb. 'Let's go for a stroll to start the digestive processes.'

Side by side they went to the cliff edge and walked along it, away from the tall finger of the lighthouse. Tina, straying close to the brink, won herself a mild rebuke from her companion, who took hold of her hand and pulled her back; when they continued on their way, he did not relinquish the hand, nor did Tina withdraw it.

At the end of a spur of cliff that pointed straight out over the sea, she pulled him with her till, like her, his toes were just over the granite edge, and they could look down to the waves breaking among the black fangs of granite like tumbled teeth of dead monsters two hundred feet and more below.

'You're not scared of heights?' he asked.

'No. I only ever had one phobia,' said Tina, 'and my well-wishing unknown friend cured me of that the hard way. Do heights trouble you, Tom?'

'Scare me silly,' he replied.

They went back to their picnic spot and packed things away in the boot of the car. By the time they left the sky was overcast and the first white horses were beginning to ruffle the sea's bland calmness; the Plymouth-bound yacht was collecting foam under her sharp stem and heeling gracefully before the gathering wind.

When Cobb had negotiated the winding lanes back to Trepoll Haven and delivered Tina to her door the wind had increased to a half-gale that bent the palm trees in its mounting fury, and the seabirds were winging their way over the clifftop and heading inland.

'Don't forget to ring your chum at Scotland Yard, Tina,' he reminded her.

'I wón't,' she replied, and gave him her cheek to kiss. 'It was a lovely afternoon, Tom. I really needed that.'

Eight

There was no dusk. By six o'clock, the sky was black with overcast, never to clear before night took over: a night of nature's high frenzy, where the sea was whipped into total whiteness, where the giant combers lashed at the very foot of the cliffs and sent spray over the crest, even splattering the windows of the cottage with salty droplets; and the wind screamed in the rafters, while the rain bucketed down almost horizontally, driven to madness by the monstrous south-wester.

At about eight o'clock, Tina telephoned Cobb.

'Heavens, Tom – what a night! How are you managing in St Costello?'

'The street outside's running in rain water like a mountain stream,' he said. 'How are you making out at Clifftop?'

'I'm expecting the roof to take off any minute, and the wind makes it difficult to hear oneself think.'

'Did you ring Arkwright?' he asked.

'That's what I'm calling you about. All I get's a recorded voice saying that the lines to London are engaged and please try again later. Whether it's normal heavy traffic or the storm's blown the lines down, one can only surmise. But something's just occurred to me. . . .'

'What's that, Tina?'

'Silly of me – but, though I really retain a very poor visual impression of the features on the severed head, I suddenly remembered that I have cast-iron evidence as to identity. . . .'

'What?'

'Teeth, of course! And the victim – Duke, or whoever he was – must certainly have spent some time, and money, in a

125

dentist's chair, what with gold fillings, splints, bridgework That mouth cost a fortune and has to be well-documented in some dentist's files.'

'Of course!' he sounded animated. 'As good as fingerprints and easier to read! Have you not told Arkwright about this already?'

'No, it slipped my mind, but I'll have another shot a ringing him at home later – okay?'

'Fine.'

'See you later. Don't get wet. And, once again, thanks for a lovely picnic. And please thank your mother for me.'

The early equinoctial gales of that particular year were destined to supplant most other recent entries in the textbooks as regards the continued intensity of wind force, the volume of rainfall, the totally unremitting darkness that turned day into night for over sixty hours non-stop.

Tina was correct in her guess that the telephone lines to London were all down, and her call to Cobb was among the last between Trepoll Haven and its market town for many days. Nor was that the only line of communication to be broken between the village and the outer world: the River Tullet, which in happier times meandered down the shallow valley through which also ran the St Costello road where Nancy Chambers had met her tragic end, became suddenly in spate. Fed by the torrents of rain that fell on the high ground in the Cornish hinterland, its brooks, streams and runnels poured insupportable volumes of reddish-brown flood water into the main stream. The river burst its bank half-way between town and village, spread over the farmland and habitations in the valley and effectively turned Trepoll Haven into an island by daylight – only there was no daylight.

Tina, becalmed by Cobb's prescription, slept all unaware of the frenzy without, and woke amidst darkness and great sound to find that it was already mid-morning. She got up showered and switched on the kettle to make coffee. Nothing happened. The power was off, and the lighting circuit failed soon after. Undeterred, she lit a candle and, skirmishing around the place for combustibles, found enough scraps of wood to get the antiquated solid-fuel stove in the kitchen working sufficiently to heat the water and provide a hot plate on which to boil a saucepan for drinking. She managed to make a cup of coffee in time for elevenses, and switched on the little portable radio to hear news of the storm. The battery was all but gone!

By putting the speaker close to her ear she was able to catch, faint and far away, a voice informing her that the river had flooded, telephone and electrical lines were all down, and South Cornwall had been provisionally declared a disaster area. The announcer went on to give police instructions to householders, tourists and other motorists regarding safety in the home or on the road – until his voice faded and died away as the battery gave out.

It was then that Tina was assaulted with the dreadful realization that she was entirely cut off and alone.

Yet not alone. . . .

The process by which a rational and highly intelligent woman like Doctor Tina May was reduced to a tangle of bared nerve ends may briefly be summarized: the darkness and isolation, the ever-present menace of natural forces at their most omnipotent and destructive, the by no means exaggerated supposition that so slight a structure as Clifftop Cottage might be rendered roofless by the gale-force winds, its doors and windows blown out, the very walls blasted apart – these concepts in themselves should have been enough to erode the basically cheerful and dogged-as-does-it approach with which Tina had met the initial impact of her situation.

But it was the – *other things* – that tended to sap her resolution.

In the flickering candle flame she became hideously aware

127

– more so than she had ever been – of the demonic figure that had punched its way through the wall of the living room and was now in there, with her. She moved into the study, which was both smaller and cosy with it; but though the bookcase more or less hid the mural of the blonde sacrifice, she could not fail to be aware of its lurking presence. She quit the study by the mid-afternoon and retired to the kitchen, where at least there were the homely sounds of the pot-bellied stove consuming the vast hodsful of anthracite with which she constantly had to replenish it. And there was no ghastly mural to remind her of what she did not wish to be reminded

And then she lost – time.

She had had three potential sources of time: her wristwatch the long-case clock in the sitting room, and the time check from the radio. The radio was out. She forgot to wind up the long-case clock. And her wristwatch – notoriously inaccurate – she simply disbelieved: how could it possibly be three o'clock and as black as pitch outside?

Or – was it three o'clock in the *morning*?

Nature then added a new line of instrumentation to its insane concerto of fury. This was announced by a lightning flash that seared right through the window curtains, to the kitchen where Tina May sat huddled with her umpteenth cup of coffee warming her hands; illuminating the room as brightly as full sunshine for a flickering instant – to be followed by a drum roll of thunder immediately overhead that caused Tina to upset scalding coffee over her lap and cry out at the agony of it.

The obsession that she was not alone on the clifftop was slow in coming, but having established itself in her conscious ness, would not go away. The scratching on the kitchen window which she could just hear when the wind slightly abated for a few moments – surely that was a set of taloned fingernails being scratched lightly over the panes as a sort of summons to her. When she elicited, by means of her pocket torch, that it was no more than a branch of ivy trailing against the window, she derived little comfort from the knowledge

128

for straight away she was faced with the hideous question of who was it rattling the handle of the solarium's outer door? It proved to be the wind, but that brought her little consolation. Each false alarm perversely confirmed her in the view that someone – or some people – were lurking in the darkness of the garden, prowling around outside the cottage and waiting for an opportunity to gain admission.

The night – day? – wore on. The thunderstorm passed over, but was quickly succeeded by another. She tried the radio again, but it gave out only the ghostly outline of wailing violins that faded into the silence of finality.

She opened a tin of soup and warmed it through on the stove top; took a few spoonsful, then laid it aside. By her watch she then decided that she had had enough of the menacing solitude of Clifftop Cottage, and resolved to get out – anywhere – to rid herself of the risk of madness that might come upon her if she were further pressured by – say – whoever it was who had terrorized her with the snake phobia. The watch said seven, though to which seven neither her sleep pattern and appetite, nor the state of the sky outside, offered the slightest clue.

Get out – that's what she would do!

There was, she knew, a one-star hotel in the village: a former manor house, much decayed, that dominated the rising ground at the far side of the main street. There must also be boarding houses, and private homes which catered for down-market tourists with bed and breakfast. Any of these would suit her: all she craved for was light, warmth, a bit of company – and some contact with the world outside the narrow compass that she could discern through the storm-lashed windows of Clifftop Cottage.

The resolution made, she put it into operation: went up to the bedroom and crammed a change of linen and a spare skirt and jumper into her overnight bag, along with washing gear, make-up and sleeping pills. She slipped on her mackintosh, tied a headscarf firmly under her chin. And contemplated on her means of transport.

The bicycle, definitely. Her ankle still pained, and she walked with a heavy limp. The rutted, steep lane down to the village might take its toll, reducing her to lameness and near-immobility before she had found some place of asylum. She had a mental image of herself marooned, helpless, half-way down the lane, with the furies of the night tearing into her, reducing her to a prostrate, quivering mass of helplessness.

One last look round the kitchen and the solarium and, blowing out the candle, she unlocked and opened the outer back door – and was instantly assaulted by the full force of the gale that sent her reeling back into the cottage, and then, when the furious wind drew breath, sucked out into the tortured night like a cork from a bottle. The door slammed behind her. She had the presence of mind to lock it, and then, hefting her overnight bag, and probing the darkness ahead with the thin beam of her pocket torch, made her painful way in the general direction of the small tool shed at the corner of the garden, where she had housed the bicycle.

Blessedly, she found the shed, wrenched open the door and wheeled out the cycle, hooking her bag over the handlebars. She had not pushed the machine more than a few yards preparative to mounting it before she was struck by the difficulty she had in shoving it along.

She flashed the torch beam over the machine, probing at its moving parts, in anticipation of finding something – a piece of string perhaps – caught up in the wheel spokes.

No such thing. The fault lay with the tyres: they had been slashed open like gutted fish!

In her sudden confusion, she dropped the torch, which was immediately extinguished. There was no such item fitted to the bicycle – which was useless anyhow – so she went down on both knees and scrabbled for the torch among the long grass, praying for a lightning flash to come and guide her hand.

Her prayer was granted: fingers closing round the shaft of the torch as a distant glare briefly touched the shiny metal, she juggled with the switch.

Nothing happened. It was broken.

No bicycle. No torch. Alone and helpless in the night of screaming wind and driving rain. Her will sagged to submission. She was beaten. Even the solitude of beleaguered Clifftop Cottage had an allure, compared with the inhospitable night. Detaching her overnight bag, she left the bike where it lay and stumbled back to the cottage door, digging into her mack pocket for the key to open up again.

The key was not there: she must have fumbled and dropped it.

Back on her hands and knees again, Tina felt about for the key, and the nettles in the rank grass stung her fingers intolerably; but the wretched thing – and it was big enough in all conscience – was nowhere to be found.

Not only bereft of every means to get away, she no longer had the option of retreat!

Still kneeling, and teetering close to real despair, Tina stared up into the darkness and the scudding low clouds, the rain lashing her face like a cat o' nine tails, each tail loaded with a pinpoint of lead shot.

'Help me – someone please help me!' she breathed.

The next bolt of lightning lit her whole world from the zenith downwards, rending the low clouds and describing their puffy shapes, illuminating each individual slanting stream of rain, touching every blade of grass, every leaf and branch on the clifftop. It encompassed the cottage, roof and gutterings, windows and their frames, each dab of cement in the interstices of the stonework, the lichen growing on the southern side. With its great light, it revealed the beginning of the lane leading on past the cottage and down towards the village.

It described the tall figure that was lurching towards her up the lane, seemingly impervious to wind and rain. She saw every detail of its lineaments.

She saw the horned goat's head, the flashing eyes.

Blind panic is misnamed; there is no blindness in the frantic
131

desire to escape, only a certain over-haste that is mistaken for confusion.

The supercharge of adrenaline that informed Tina's reaction clearly defined her two options of escape, which lay either down the staircase to the beach, or through the gate in the garden fence and out along the clifftop. She chose the latter because it offered more opportunities for concealment among the gorse and shrubbery, and also because it held out the hope of eventual access to the village street.

The decision made, she was already at the gate and through it before the demonic intruder could have advanced round the side of the cottage.

Darkness was her ally: given the head start she had, there was no reason why she should not so distance herself from her pursuer (she had already reckoned the thing as her pursuer) as to be in no real danger whatsoever. And she knew, as well as she then lived and breathed, that the thing's coming was a threat to her very life.

A dozen swift strides beyond the fence she looked back, straining her eyes against the total darkness that was also shrouded in a curtain of blinding rain. Nothing there. The thing could not have seen her line of escape; must now be standing, irresolute, somewhere near the corner of the cottage, trying to determine which way she had gone (since it was obvious that, she having seen the creature with the goat head, it must also have seen her).

There came another searing flash of lightning. And during the tremendous crash that accompanied it, she saw the hideous intruder – now her slayer to be – standing not six paces from where she stood, having already passed through the gate in the fence!

One look, and she was running – with the vision of the staring eyes, and the bared teeth in the grinning mouth, burning in the forefront of her brain.

Terror lent wings to her flying feet, but not for long. Stumbling badly on the craggy path, she turned her ankle over and suffered a sudden agony from her wound and the assaulted muscles surrounding it. When next she put the foot to the ground, she was limping heavily.

Blessedly, the darkness persisted. She had no thought to look behind her again, for it would avail her nothing; likewise, the thing coming after could have no idea if it was near or far from its prey.

Unless – and the thought nearly choked her – *unless it possessed superhuman powers of perception!*

The very thought spurred her on; disregarding the mounting agony of her ankle, she struck out with a new, desperate vigour – all the time expecting the feel of a taloned hand upon her shoulder, bringing her, spinning, to a halt. Her very impetus dictated what happened next: she tripped over a tangled root and was impelled sideways by the force of her onward rush, clean off the narrow path – to plunge, face-forwards, into a prickly mattress of gorse, which received her into its wet maw and closed about her in concealment.

Total darkness. And nothing to hear but the screaming of the wind and her own heartbeats as she lay there.

Slowly and with infinite caution she turned her head sideways against the accommodating gorse and peered back over her shoulder. There was nothing to be seen, but the creature could not be far away. In the brief time since her fall, its running footsteps could not have taken it more than a few paces; but even that contained the seeds of a blessing; she had only to wait, not move, let a little time go by, and she would be free of the menace.

Lie still, girl, and stay calm.

Another lightning flash destroyed her high hopes. . . .

The thing was standing not five paces from her, on the path, looking to right and left, looking for her. She ceased to breathe, now there was only the thud-thud of a vein in her temple marking off a passing lifetime.

Tina closed her eyes. And thought she heard footsteps starting up again.

Were they coming towards her? She felt herself begin to die.

Opening her eyes to meet her fate, she saw with a sudden lurch of the heart that the thing was moving away from her; walking slowly down the path, in clear view from a spate of smaller lightning flashes that seemed to be chorusing together in the dark clouds above, accompanied by a constant drum roll of thunder. It was then that the thin possibility of escape came to her. Half-crouched, half-lying with her cheek against the harsh gorse fronds, she screwed her mind to a feverish calculation of her chances. Let the thing be out of sight when the next major lightning flash lit up the clifftop – and then creep away, across the flattened crest in the direction of the village street – no more than fifty yards – then to slither down the steep slope. . . .

How far away was it now? The lightning flashes had ceased, but the creature was not beyond the compass of her vision, surely. Not yet. And perhaps it had crossed what passed for its mind that she might be hidden here among the gorse.

In which case, it would come back! The horror of that was not to be thought about; best thrust it to one side. Wait – and hope.

After an eternity of waiting the heavens were split by just such a fork of lightning as the one which had first revealed the intruder in the lane, so that her vision was unimpeded as far as the eye could perceive.

To her heartfelt relief, the clifftop was empty. The thing had passed on, no doubt at a tremendous rate, in order – as it thought – to overtake its victim.

Cautiously, still half-fearful that she may have been mistaken, Tina raised herself up and began a slow and painful limp towards the landward edge of the clifftop. It was further than she thought; but eventually she could discern the pinpoints of faint light that revealed the clustered buildings of Trepoll Haven.

She presently came to where the ground fell sharply away, down to the road that passed somewhere below her. The surface of the slope was of crumbled sandstone dotted with clumps of the ubiquitous gorse. Seizing hold of one of these, she gingerly eased herself down into a sitting position, feet extended – and let herself go, checking her downward progress, as best she was able, by grabbing at any gorse fronds that came within reach; but she had precious little control over her descent into the darkness and suffered bruises and lacerated hands along the way till at length she tumbled into a torrent of rain water pouring along the edge of the main street.

Picking herself unsteadily to her feet, Tina decided to set her course towards a lighted window that showed ahead through the rain, and limped painfully towards it, arms extended to fend off unseen obstacles. Presently her hands closed on a gate, which she was able to unlatch and pass through. There was a door ahead of her, marked by an oval-shaped fanlight above; on tottering steps, she edged towards it. When she reached out to touch the streaming woodwork, she overbalanced and fell heavily.

Her head connected, stunningly, with the kerbing of a garden path, and she was pitched into unconsciousness.

'Ah, my dear young lady – not so badly hurt as we had thought. What a blessing.'

The voice was unmistakable, the setting unfamiliar. She was lying on someone's sofa with a rug over her. As far as she could determine, most if not all of her wet clothes had been removed, and she felt pleasantly warm and cosseted.

'Doctor Strang. . . .' She murmured the name, looking up at his dramatically handsome old countenance.

'You picked a providentially convenient spot to collapse,' he said. 'Mr and Mrs Wicks heard you cry out. Happily, I live only three doors further along from here. But, my dear Dr May, what were you doing out in such weather as this? And the *state* that you were in – bless my soul!'

Two figures hovered in the background of the small, cosy room: a middle-aged man and wife, rosy-cheeked and homely-looking; nothing to worry about there; nevertheless she was wary, and did not reply to Strang's leading question.

The latter indicated the couple: 'These are your hosts, my dear young lady – Mr and Mrs Wicks do bed and breakfast, but had scarcely expected to have a customer on such a night as this.' The concept seemed to amuse him.

'Such a pleasure, Doctor May.' The woman was gently gushing, and the man blinked with embarrassed pleasure behind his steel-rimmed spectacles. 'We never miss your programme, do we Eric?'

'Not never,' averred her spouse.

'Well, my dears,' said Strang, addressing the pair, 'if you will excuse me, I should like to make a thorough examination of my patient to determine if she has harmed herself in any way. Do you mind? . . .'

Obedient to his smile and gesture, they backed away and out of the room, bobbing their heads as if leaving the presence of royalty.

'Splendid folk,' said Strang when the door closed behind them. 'You'd best stay here, I think, till the weather abates. I take it that you have lost all your main services up there in Clifftop?'

She nodded.

He sat down at the sofa at her feet; fixed her with a quizzical glance.

'Now then, what's amiss?' he asked. 'You have the looks and manner of a person who's seen the proverbial ghost. Out with it, my dear – what have you been up to?'

Pausing only for a few moments to order her thoughts and to decide upon how to spell out her dreadful story, Tina then told him everything that had happened in as straightforward, plain and unvarnished a manner as she was able. The old man was very sympathetic when she spoke of the succession of small disasters which, taken all together, added up to the intolerable situation that had driven her out of Clifftop Cottage to seek shelter elsewhere.

When she came to arrival of the goat-headed thing, his

reactions grew less sympathetic, more – withdrawn from her.

'Undoubtedly a tramp,' was his conclusion. 'A vagrant of the roads, denied, no doubt, his usual rough shelter for the night, and driven to beg for a crust and somewhere dry to lay his head. There are many such in these parts.'

'If a tramp, he was of uncommonly odd appearance,' said Tina dryly.

But the old man had a formula for that: 'On such a night, with lightning, torrential rain and a gale of wind, the eye can set up deceptive patterns in the mind,' he said, and seemed to think that he had adequately explained the phenomenon of the goat-headed menace.

Tina had an impulse to pursue the argument; but decided to let it pass.

'Well now,' he said with a hearty 'we've got that over with, and now to work' manner. 'Let's have a look at those bruises which, considering the torn state of your garments, must be fairly widespread. And your hands – tch, tch! Not a fingernail unscathed!

Meekly, Tina submitted herself to his gentle ministrations. He called for Mrs Wicks to bring boiled water and himself bathed her cuts and bruises, being particularly concerned over her beautifully shaped hands and fingernails – now lacerated, torn, and ingrained with the grime of rough passage. Next, he disinfected the wounds and dressed them with lint and bandages. When the last careful bow had been tied he sat back and admired his handiwork.

'And now,' he said, 'I suppose you're going to demand the name of the miscreant who almost certainly put that adder through your letter box?'

'I think the time's come when I simply must know,' responded Tina. 'There have been so many appalling happenings since I arrived in Trepoll Haven that I feel I've simply got to get to the truth of it all – if only to clear myself of the idiotic suspicions that are flying around me.'

'Then I will tell all I know,' declared Strang.

137

'Lenny Jordan is your man.'

The declaration did not strike home to Tina till she had given some thought to the name and where she had heard it before.

'You mean the very powerful-looking young man who works at the holiday camp?' she said.

'That's right,' said the other. 'He mows the grass and tends to the flower beds, acts as lavatory cleaner, odd-job man and general factotum. Also looks after the swimming pool.'

'And you think it was he who hung the dead snakes from the door knocker and pushed the live one through the letter box?'

'Not Lenny's first essay into that particular act of nastiness,' said Strang. 'He's a man with all his physical faculties, and quite cunning in the manner of the simple-minded, but he was brain-damaged at birth and his critical faculties are impaired to a degree. When he was a young lad of about eight or nine, he took against a member of this community and played the selfsame trick of slipping an adder through the offender's letter box. Happily, in that particular case, no one was bitten. But – yes, I would say that you have somehow angered him, and in his simple and unthinking manner, he took revenge on you.'

'When I was called to Mrs Wakeley,' said Tina, remembering, 'he was frantically trying to revive her, though it was obvious at a glance that she was dead. To humour him, because he was obviously so concerned, I stood aside and let him carry on for quite a while. Even then, I fancy, he felt that I hadn't given him every last chance to save her. He must have thought very highly of her to. . . .'

She paused, glanced sharply at Strang. He nodded.

'He was undoubtedly Glenda Wakeley's lover,' he said.

'A hobbledehoy like *him*?' Tina stared at her companion in blank disbelief. 'Man-mad she may have been, but surely not – indiscriminate?'

138

Strang sighed. 'Her taste was of the catholic sort,' he said. 'And she displayed a distinct liking for male flesh which is of the earth, earthy.'

After a while she said: 'You realize that, according to the theory that Tom Cobb and I ad-libbed together, Glenda Wakeley died as a result of a lovers' quarrel – in which case Lenny's probably our man?'

He nodded. 'I appreciate that, and gave the matter a lot of thought before telling you what I know.'

Tina leaned back against her pillow and closed her eyes, behind which she tried to reassemble the image of the man Lenny Jordan on the one occasion when she had met him: the giant of a man with angry, close-set eyes and a surly, truculent manner; but the image would not harden, for all that came out was a mental image of a similar, hulking shape silhouetted against the lightning flash, with the hideous head which must have been a mask.

Nine

Tina stayed at the Wicks' till it was all over.

After what had been, in effect, three consecutive nights, daylight came again on the Saturday morning: a thin, unsatisfying daylight, chill and apologetic; but it brought people out of doors to savour the still vicious wind, to contemplate the flooded pastures in the valley, the swollen streams, the angry waves that swept right over the breakwater of Trepoll Haven at high tide.

That afternoon Tina returned to Clifftop Cottage to find that the electricity had been restored. Not so the telephone. She would have stopped off at the stores to buy a battery for her portable radio, but mindful of the treatment she had received from Penlee the proprietor, she gave it a miss.

Back in the cottage, she took stock of her situation and decided that the best thing she could do would be to cut her losses (which in simply pecuniary terms had been negligible), pack up and go home at the earliest opportunity, and the hell with her 'retreat'. But it would have been a polite elegance to have been able to ring Dermot Heymans and tell him first.

She had got around to making a pot of tea when she heard a car coming up the drive. Peering out of the window she was in time to see Detective Inspector Wainhouse approaching her door. She opened it in his face before he could knock – always disconcerting.

'Good afternoon, Mr Wainhouse,' she said. 'This is an unexpected visit.'

Did she detect a certain softening of his manner, a distinct shamefacedness in his approach? She thought she did.

He took the seat that she indicated for him; seemed hardly

140

to know what to do with his hat, crossed and re-crossed his legs several times and never to his satisfaction. Finally, he fixed her with a bovine stare and said: 'I've called to ask for your help, Doctor. We need you badly.'

'Really?' she asked, surprised. 'Well, of course I'll help in any way I can. But – how?'

He said: 'We've got six bodies – all drowned folk, save one who was under a tree that was struck by lightning. And we haven't found the crew of a yacht that foundered in the bay on Thursday night when the storm began. And there's others missing, of course – as you'll have heard.'

Tina thought of the yacht that had been shaping course past Dorwell Head on the afternoon of the picnic.

'We wondered at headquarters if you'd carry out the necessary post mortems, Doctor,' said Wainhouse. 'There being no one else but you in the vicinity, like. . . .' He paused, looking at her appealingly.

'But – what about Doctor Cobb?' asked Tina. 'Oh, what am I saying? He can't possibly cope with all that, single-handed. Yes, of course I'll be glad to help. . . .

'Why are you staring at me, Mr Wainhouse?' she demanded.

He looked grave, and he had the face for it. 'Didn't you know, ma'am?' he asked. 'Doctor Cobb's missing – that's to say his body's not turned up. . . .'

'Oh, no!'

'They found his car on the road when the river went down,' said Wainhouse. 'It had been completely inundated when the torrent broke its banks. The driver's door was open, so he'd made an attempt to swim for it I guess. But – well, he never made it to safety.'

'How awful!' Tina crossed over to the window and looked out over the blustery landscape of village and valley, unwilling to display her sense of shock and loss to the detective. 'How's his mother taking it?' she asked.

'I don't know,' replied the other. 'Badly, I 'spect. Luckily, it wasn't in my department to break the news to her.' He stood up to go. 'Well, thanks for rallying round, Doctor,' he said. 'The emergency mortuary's been set up at Tremayne School, and the bodies are being taken from there to the District General for the post mortems. There'll be a police car placed at your disposal from ten o'clock tomorrow. Can you be ready then?'

Tina nodded.

'Strange, isn't it?' he said. 'Nature takes a hand and drives everything else into second place. What's one death or two against a disaster of this size?

'I'm sorry about the business of that head and all that, Doctor. I – that's to say we – made all the usual inquiries through the proper channels. No ill feeling about that, I hope?'

'No ill feeling, Mr Wainhouse,' responded Tina automatically.

Glenda Wakeley and Nancy Chambers, she thought. As well as Ellis Duke, or whoever. Balance them against Tom Cobb and six others, not to mention a yacht's crew and heaven knows who else.

But is death to be measured only quantitively?

They were all, police and mortuary staff both, as gently deferential to her as it was possible to be: insisted on her taking a break after each examination. Another doctor – a houseman seconded from his hospital duties – helped with the post mortems which had by that time increased to eight, two of the yachtsmen's bodies having been washed up. But no Tom Cobb. They also gave her a very tolerable lunch in the Medical Staff restaurant and made a tremendous fuss of her; insisted on her signing the visitors' book. Two more examinations finished off the afternoon. She was glad when it was all over.

On the way back through the town, whose streets were still littered with the filth of the river's passing, she asked her amiable policewoman driver if she could drop her off for half an hour at the Cobb house, and the woman obligingly agreed.

Tina rang the bell and was answered by a young woman in an apron who looked as if she had been crying. In response to the visitor's request, she said that Mrs Cobb was at home and that if Doctor May would like to wait in the sitting room she'd go and see if Madam would receive her.

The sitting room was at the rear of the rather grand Edwardian town house, with a view out of French windows into a secluded back garden comprising a lawn with a centre feature of an ornamental stone urn set with geraniums, a well-stocked herbaceous border surrounding, and a sentinel circle of whispering cypresses shutting out the world beyond.

A coal fire burned cheerfully in a grate beneath a marble overmantel upon which nestled a whole picture gallery of photographs, groups and portraits. The centrepiece comprised a trio of large silver-framed prints showing the clearly recognizable young Mrs Cobb, looking very beautiful and quite clearly still sighted, dressed in white on her wedding day. She was on the arm of just another Tom Cobb, save that he was moustached and wearing RAF officer's uniform with wings and a row of medal ribbons. This was flanked by two pictures of Tom. On the left, Tom the schoolboy in cricket blazer and flannels, carrying a bat, looking bronzed and aggressive – as a cricketer should; and the gently contemplative Tom on the right, in academic dress, his parchment scroll in hand.

The clock at one end of the chimneypiece thinly tinkled the half-hour as the door opened and Mrs Cobb came in. As before, she was walking without the aid of a stick, and masked her blindness with a devastating accuracy of movement and a faultless directing of her eyes towards the person whom she addressed:

'Doctor May, how thoughtful of you to call. You've heard about my poor Tom, of course.'

It was not a question, merely a sober statement of fact; clearly, the woman's fortitude was of a higher order than that of the servant, thought Tina – till she came closer and saw the lines of strain and sleeplessness around the other's eyes.

'I'll ring for tea,' said Mrs Cobb. 'You'll join me, Doctor?'

'Thank you, Mrs Cobb, but I can't. The car's calling for me quite soon. I only came to offer my condolences. And I hope – one profoundly hopes. . . .'

'There's no hope – none at all,' responded the other woman. 'Tom's dead. I was with him when he died.'

Speechless in the face of this astounding statement, Tina remembered Tom Cobb's assertion that his mother had second sight. Her next remark was apposite:

'I also saw my husband die,' she said calmly. 'That's him in our wedding photo, of course.' And she pointed accurately to the centrepiece photograph. 'He was shot down in one of the last sorties of the war in Burma. His body was never found. Tom's will doubtless be recovered.

'Doctor, I should like to ask a very special favour of you.'

'Please do, Mrs Cobb,' replied Tina.

'After my Tom's body is recovered, there will, of course, have to be a post mortem. I should feel happy if you would carry out the examination. There is a fitness in it, a suitability, for Tom spoke very highly of you. Very highly. Indeed, I think that, if he had lived. . . .' She made a vague gesture, and her classically beautiful features, which had taken on a certain softness, resumed her habitual expression of serene self-containment, as if in defence against a sighted world that had best be shut out.

'Yes, of course, Mrs Cobb,' responded Tina. 'I'll do it.'

She was thankful when the police car called for her shortly afterwards, and glad to leave that house of mourning, for all that Mrs Cobb had filled in the awkward gap of waiting with bland small-talk.

The telephone line from the village to St Costello was re-established that evening; those to London and the country at large were to wait till morning.

That evening, also, a gang of council workmen operating a bulldozer in the lower part of Trepoll Haven to remove a mass of debris which had been carried down by the flooded river and deposited in the fields and cottage gardens, unearthed a significantly shaped item which, when the thick mud was washed from it, was revealed to be a human skull minus the jawbone and showing signs of charring from fire. The police were called, and the skull having been located in the garden of Lenny Jordan, who lived alone in a cottage close by the river, he was brought in and questioned as to why such an article should have been given a shallow burial in his vegetable patch.

Despite all inducements, persuasions and threats, however, Lenny was not at first forthcoming . . . .

The mail came through that evening, and with it a packet addressed to Doctor Tina May from Scotland Yard. It contained two photographs that meant nothing to her, and a brief memo from Detective Sergeant Turner:

> These are the only known photos of Ellis Duke.
> Granted that he was wearing a beard at the
> time they were taken (in Paris, about 3/4
> years ago), and that you say the severed head
> was clean-shaven, can you state positively
> that his was the head in question? Please
> communicate your answer a.s.a.p.
>
> – A.W. Turner

Dutifully addressing herself to the photographs again and again, Tina could not bring herself to making a positive answer either one way or another. For one thing, the prints were not particularly clear, they were also in black and white, so that the issue of colouring, particularly eye and hair colouring, was not to be resolved. In the end, she came down on a negative conclusion and tried to phone it through to Scotland Yard, only to be told by the local operator, who cut in, that repairs were being carried out, but that the lines to London would not be available again till morning.

Restless, Tina wandered through the cottage, puzzling her mind with questions, the answers for which – maddeningly – seemed to be only just beyond the compass of her reach.

WHO was the severed head? . . .

WHO – presuming that we do, after all, live in a rational world and that Satan is simply a metaphysical concept – pursued her on the clifftop that hideous night of the gale? . . .

WHO drowned Glenda Wakeley? . . .

WHO contrived the death of Nancy Chambers – and, by implication, Tina May? . . .

And, as a corollary to all those questions – WHY – WHY – WHY?

The answers must lie somewhere. In the cottage, perhaps? The notion struck her very forcibly. She examined the mural in the sitting room: tried to see it with a fresh eye. Did the representation exactly resemble the thing she had encountered on the clifftop? So far as the head was concerned – yes. She was less certain about the clothing, which, insofar as the figure in the painting wore vestigial garments over its hairy torso, they were of vaguely medieval style; and she had not noticed what her pursuer had been wearing.

She went into the study and, pulling the bookcase aside, regarded the sacrificial scene. The nude victim was clearly Glenda Wakeley, but what was the significance – if any – of the act of sacrificing her to the knife? The satanic figure was certainly the same as the one depicted in the sitting room.

The bathroom presented more problems, posed innumerable questions. Again, the goat-headed creature was the same. Its cavorting acolytes – nymphs, satyrs, naiads and mermen – all had neutral, stereotyped features unsuggestive of portraiture. This, to Tina, begged the question of why, if Glenda Wakeley was so frankly portrayed in the study, had the artist been so coy about depicting the true features of the remainder of his coven? She searched the faces again; and again learned nothing from the pasteboard figures and their stock, off-the-peg facial characterizations.

Why had Duke, who had not jibbed at depicting the

146

:atures of the vicar's wife, his mistress, been coy about the
lentity of the rest of the women and men involved in his
rcane practices?

She was still mulling over the mysteries, and washing up at
he kitchen sink after a supper of hastily prepared spaghetti
3olognese which she had eaten absently and with scarcely
ny post-recollection, when a knock on the door announced
he arrival again of Detective Inspector Wainhouse, now
ccompanied by PC Tuttle. The attitude of both men was
quite absurdly different from the previous occasion when
hey had called upon her together; in place of the barely
concealed contempt, there was now a humility, a distinct air
of apology, almost a desperation to make amends and to
prove to her that she was a valued consultant in the
unravelling of the mysteries that bedevilled – almost literally
pedevilled – the peace and quiet of Trepoll Haven.

'Doctor, we've brought something for you to look at,'
volunteered Wainhouse by way of a conversational opening.
Tuttle, just you lay it down here on the table.

'With your permission, ma'am,' he added.

'It' was a middling-sized, square cardboard box. Almost
before they opened it up, Tina had a premonition of what it
must contain; Tuttle's involuntary grimace of distaste when
he glanced inside the box confirmed her hunch.

Not the severed head, but the domed top of a skull, met her
gaze when she looked, and without hesitation lifted it out.
The jawbone, released of the connective tissues had, of
course, fallen away and was not in the box. The bone was
blackened, scarred and pitted by fire, and some of the thinner
portions entirely consumed. What had not been touched in
any regard were the teeth; except for where the cunningly
wrought gold bridgework of the upper jaw had melted in
places, allowing the false molars to become detached. Some of
the gold fillings, also, had come away – but by no means all.

'Well, Doctor – recognize it?' asked Wainhouse.

'It's the severed head – *my* severed head,' replied Tina.
'The teeth are the give-away.'

147

There was a concerted exhalation of breath from the tw
men.

'It struck me that they might be,' said Wainhouse. 'A bit
sort of – unique, aren't they, ma'am?'

'One can't be right all the time,' said Derek Arkwright to hi
assistant, by way of consolation. 'It still remains a very goo
premise and we did right to act on it.'

Early next morning at Scotland Yard, Arkwright an
Turner got news of the skull that Tina May had matched u
with the severed head she claimed to have seen. With this
also, arrived her negative response to the photographs of Elli
Duke. Taken in conjunction, both of these facts still did no
totally exclude the possibility that both head and skull wer
remains of the mad artist of Trepoll Haven.

But one other item of information had come up overnight
and it was this which had shot Turner's theory to pieces. . .

'That's as may be, sir,' said the latter, in response to hi
chief's commiseration, 'but it puts us right back where we
were when Doctor May reported the severed head. *We* neve
did doubt her word – and all that the discovery of the skull'
done is to vindicate her to the doubters. We *still* don't know
who the guy was!'

Arkwright inclined his head in acknowledgement of th
truth of his subordinate's logic, and thoughtfully re-read the
portion of the telex which had just arrived on his desk. It wa
from Paris.

INQUIRIES OF DENTAL PRACTITIONERS IN PARIS AREA REVEAL
ELLIS KINGSMEAD DUKE UNDERWENT EXTRACTION OF UPPER
RIGHT AND LEFT INCISORS NUMBERS ONE AND TWO STOF
TEETH REPLACED BY DENTURE STOP GENERAL CONDITION OF
TEETH RECORDED AS POOR = COMMISSAIRE DE PLESSIS DE LA
SURETE NATIONALE

'In other words,' said Turner, voicing his thoughts, 'Duke
had false clackers – and the gap in his four front teeth would
148

ave been the first thing that Doctor May would have
oticed.

'What next, sir?'

Arkwright sat back in his swivel chair and rubbed his jaw.
Not for the first time, Turner speculated how his chief would
ave carried the role of a university don with consummate
ase – he with his heavy black library glasses, his air of keen
ntelligence and reflective calm.

'I think,' said Arkwright at length, 'that we go back to our
beginnings and comb through the missing persons' file.
Maybe our man came from further afield than Cornwall, or
even the West Country. He could have been a tourist, or
imply on holiday in or around Trepoll Haven.

'Get on to the local hotels. Try that holiday camp where
hey discovered the woman drowned in the swimming pool.
Find out if anyone who checked in never got around to
checking out. The deep-frozen head gave us a preconception
about the man. Maybe the head was deep frozen only the day
before Tina May saw it – in which case the victim was alive
and walking around this time last week.

'Maybe he had a car and was using some hotel as a base
while he toured around Devon and Cornwall for two or three
days on end, returning to base from time to time for a rest and
a change of clothing. Just the kind of style for a well-heeled
single man of mature years. In such a case the hotel
management might only just have got around to wondering
what happened to him.

'Oh, and check with the local constabulary for any cars
found abandoned in the area.'

Turner went off to do his chief's bidding. He paused at the
door.

'I take it we still haven't been officially called in on the
case?' he asked.

Arkwright nodded. 'True enough – but I have a nod and a
wink from the deputy chief constable that we won't be
treading on anyone's toes.

'Oh – and Turner . . .' he added.

149

'Sir?'

'One point we and the local boys might lose sight of fro[m] time to time. . . .'

'And what's that, Mr Arkwright?'

'Find why that severed head was delivered to Cliffto[n] Cottage and all the other answers will fall into place!'

There follows the transcript of a tape recording made durin[g] the interviewing of Leonard ('Lenny') Jordan, of Riversid[e] Cottage, Trepoll Haven, Cornwall and Detective Inspect[or] D.J. Wainhouse of Devon and Cornwall Constabulary, [in] connection with the discovery of a skull buried in Jordan['s] garden:

Question:	Now, Lenny, you know your rights, they've bee[n] explained to you. Why not make the most of you[r] opportunity and clear yourself of any possibl[e] charge by telling us exactly how that skull came t[o] be buried in your garden?
Answer:	I've told you again and again, I don't know.
Q:	Nor you don't know who the dead man was?
A:	No.
Q:	But you know that it was a *man's* skull – how do you kno[w] that?
A:	I don't!
Q:	But you just said so. (To the W.P.C. operating the tap[e] recorder) Play that last bit back. (This was done.)
A:	You're trying to trick me.
Q:	Was it Mr Duke – the skull?
A:	He died months ago, didn't he? Never found the body, the[y] didn't.
Q:	But you knew him, Lenny – you knew Duke well, didn['t] you?
A:	(After some hesitation) Yeah, I knew him.
Q:	You knew him well. You were a member of what he calle[d] his 'coven'.
A:	NO! (vehemently)

150

Q: I've got a sworn statement here from someone who says that you were. . . .

A: WHO TOLD YOU THAT? (angrily)

Q: Meg Chambers. She was speaking as a fellow member of the coven.

A: Meg? That lying, twisting (obscenity).

Q: And you're still a member, aren't you, Lenny? In fact, after Mr Duke was drowned, you took over from him and became – what was it Meg Chambers called you? – 'The Chief Wizard'.

A: So what? We was minding our own business and doing no harm.

Q: Do you call putting a live adder through Doctor May's letter box 'Doing no harm'?

A: Who told you that – who else you been talking to?

Q: Never you mind.

A: Only one feller could pin that one on me – and he'd better look out. Just as soon as I get out of this (obscenity) cop-shop, I'll (obscenity) him!

Q: Is that all part of minding your own business and doing no harm, Lenny?

A: You're twisting my words, trying to trick me again. I'm not saying that we're all perfect in the coven. There's one, at least, who joined for what he could get.

Q: For what he could get – what was that, Lenny?

A: What? Why, for the women, of course. All right – Mr Duke, he taught us what's called the Dio-Dionysiac rituals, which is sex and all that. But it was only part of the magic. This guy I'm talking about, he only joined for the sex. That's why his wife left him when she found out.

Q: What's his name, Lenny?

A: (laughing) You should know, Inspector.

Q: Don't fool around – his name, Lenny?

A: That copper of yours – Bert Tuttle.

Q: You're mighty free with your accusations, Jordan – do you realize what you're saying?

A: Sure. Everybody's squealing and grassing on Lenny, so I'm only getting my own back. Sure – your Bert Tuttle's with the coven – right up to his greasy neck!

(Recording ends.)

*

The morning following, when it became general knowledge
in the village that Police Constable Tuttle had been
suspended, Tina went for a walk down to the harbour, and
was most conscious of the atmosphere which pervaded the
place. The sunny weather had returned and with it the
tourists and the day trippers from the inland areas, as a result
of which W. Penlee, General Stores, was doing a roaring
trade in ice cream, children's buckets and spades, films,
postcards and the seaside comestibles so beloved by the
British.

Yet over all there hung a cloud of fear.

Tina, who prided herself on being hard-nosed, not to say
unimaginative in many regards, sensed it at once.

The thing manifested itself in the almost total absence of
locals from the streets. There was the old fellow looking after
the car park on the piece of waste ground behind the church;
one or two fishermen were to be seen mending their nets down
by the harbour wall; a few boats, indeed, had put out, but
they did not venture far and were soon back. But if the folk of
Trepoll Haven were not to be seen out, they more than
compensated by their very tangible presence behind net
curtains. Tina was embarrassingly conscious of the eyes that
probed her and took her apart from behind every curtained
window in the main street, and uncomfortably aware that her
role in the mysteries that were quietly tearing Trepoll Haven
apart behind locked doors was the source of much speculation
– most of it hostile. Well might the villagers say that it was her
arrival – she, the 'foreigner' – which had coincided with the
beginning of it all; ergo – she was the cause.

The walk resulting in only unease and embarrassment,
Tina soon returned to Clifftop, where she made yet another
attempt to reach Derek Arkwright by phone – her third try of
the morning – only to be told again that the superintendent
and Sergeant Turner were still at a meeting. She flirted with
the notion of ringing Dermot Heymans, but the bad news

152

about Tom Cobb and all else had driven the idea of cutting and running from her mind, so she felt inclined to leave Heymans till she had some firm news about her immediate plans.

Meanwhile she felt very much in a limbo: much to be done, many questions to be asked, many answers needed; but nothing happening.

Two hours to go till lunch. She had finished her seventh reading of *Two Cities*. She had nothing to do. She felt rather sticky and grubby – so she decided to have a bath. Make a nice relaxing change from the inevitable shower.

Five minutes later she was relaxed in the cosseting warmth with her favourite bath salts spilling giant bubbles all over the floor. She leaned back and contemplated the nearest mural, which was inches from her fingertips. It depicted a section of the beach, a line of rock pools, and about half a dozen naked and near-naked revellers disporting themselves.

In close-up, at her protracted leisure, she was able to examine and absorb the technique of painting which Duke had employed in the mural. Johnny Kettle had been a keen and talented amateur painter and had instructed her in some of the finer points of execution. She had an inkling of what 'glazes' and 'scumbles', 'impasto' and 'Tonking' were all about: she had a nodding acquaintance with chiaroscuro and sfumato – even if she could not draw a straight line herself.

Duke's technique, as she interpreted it, had been to sketch out the whole composition in a thin scumble of paint and then build up the main masses with thicker paint, amending the colours and tones with semi-transparent glazes almost like watercolour over the required areas, finishing off with showy impasto work – paint as thick as toothpaste, straight from the tube, often laid on with a trowel-like palette knife – to render clouds, draperies, foliage, and such areas where fine drawing was not at a premium. It was the basic, middle-of-the-road technique perfected by the old masters since the seventeenth century, the method of Van Dyck, Rubens and Rembrandt, Goya, Gainsborough and Hogarth; very effective in the hands of an expert and, though offering plenty of opportunities for bravura showing off, a technique that is determinately academic and – considering the personality of Ellis Duke, surprisingly – not avant-garde.

It was while lying there and contemplating the mural that Tina lit upon an anomaly which she might have missed entirely if her acquaintance with the work had been limited to innumerable brief glimpses of the sort that murals so often get.

She took another look – and gave it some thought.

The heads in the picture had been rendered in a different technique from the rest of the bodies.

Instead of having been begun in tightly-drawn scumble carefully overpainted with glazes – the way in which Duke had tackled the subtleties and complexities of the naked forms – the heads and faces were rather summarily dashed off in impasto paint. Almost like – afterthoughts.

She took another, closer, look at the head of a naiad who was laughingly struggling in the arms of a grinning satyr. The paint on her cheek was so thick that it had crumbled at the edge of the jawline. Reaching up, Tina slipped a fingernail under the paint. A flake of it broke off and fell away.

What she saw then had her leaping out of the bath to find her nail file. She returned with it – and recklessly scraped the impasto from the rest of the naiad's face – to disclose the homely, bucolic countenance of Meg Chambers!

Almost without pausing, she attacked the head of the grinning satyr. Once again the top layer of paint offered only the slightest resistance – and under the neutral features were those of Penlee of the general stores!

Having begun, there was no stopping. Her nail file went from one to the other of the figures, scratching and scraping away the impasto to reveal that each original head and every set of features had been painted with the same meticulous technique as the rest of the body, and then summarily overpainted at a later date with what amounted to a concealing mask!

Most of the original faces, though lifelike to a remarkable degree, were unknown to her; but she uncovered several that were horribly familiar:

Mrs Slyte, neighbour to Tuttle the policeman – Tuttle himself – the Penlee woman – Hargreaves from the holiday camp – Lenny. . . .

And, close up in the foreground, the image of evil itself, made human in the grinning lewdness of a countenance that made her throw aside the nail file and rush out to the telephone.

Once again, neither Arkwright nor Turner was available to speak to her, but would Doctor May care to leave a message?

Yes, Doctor May would. . . .

'Tell Detective Superintendent Arkwright or Detective Sergeant Turner to ring me, please, immediately they return.

'Tell them it's urgent – a matter of life and death!'

Ten

To John Steerforth and his fellow volunteer coastguardman
Nick Pendragon fell the unenviable task, that day, of scouring
the beaches, the rocks and the water pools for bodies. One o
the yacht's crew was still unaccounted for, together with a
child and two males who had been washed out to sea during
the flooding of the valley, and hopes were fading for the
recovery of their remains; as so often happened in that stretch
of the coast, the phenomenal tides bore away the majority of
its victims to the trackless wastes of the Atlantic; but for the
sake of the bereaved, for the sake of human dignity, the task
had to be done.

It was fast approaching high tide. The spindrift at the
landward edge of the encroaching sea was already wind
driven right up the beach to the foot of the great granite cliffs
Half a mile or so further on a line of steps cut into the rock
marked the last chance for the two coastguardmen to climb
up out of the beach to safety before they were engulfed by the
tide. When the first of the spent breakers came high enough to
wash the caked sand and shingle from the soles of his stout
kneeboots, Steerforth nodded to his companion and both
quickened their pace.

'This is about it, Johnny,' said Pendragon.

'I'll ring through when we get back and tell 'em there'll be
no more bodies showing,' replied the other. 'Davy Jones has
got the lot now.'

The two men were cutting it mighty fine: the incoming tide
would, by their expert reckoning, be knee deep by the time
they reached the steps, and thank God there was no power in
the waves, though even now a freak squall could blow up in
the next few minutes, have them soaked through and in real

azard before they were safe. Both had been caught out that
vay before.

'Step lively, Nick,' grunted Steerforth. 'Last man ashore
uys the beer.'

His companion grinned and quickened his pace also. They
ad not gone much further before a crescent shape of water,
urging ahead of the rest, cut right across their path fifty yards
head and, striking a tumbled mass of broken rocks at the
ase of the cliff, disintegrated in a high flurry of white water.
Almost at the same time, Steerforth felt a sharp gust of wind
an his left cheek – the one facing seaward. Turning his head,
e saw the white horses rising in serried ranks out beyond the
hird wave – and already they were breaking off in spindrift.

'It's a squall, Nick!' he cried. 'Run for it!'

They quickened to a steady, plodding jog-trot which was
bout their best pace with heavy boots in the yielding sand.
There was still a piece to go – five hundred yards or more.
And now the squall was driving on the sea till it covered half
he beach in patches, right up to the cliff. They were going to
;et their trousers wet, if nothing worse.

The wind increased in strength, and now the men were
unning into it, leaning forward against its implacable force.
Moreover, they were splashing, calf-deep, all the time. It
assed through Pendragon's mind that, if he should fall and
reak an ankle, his older and less robust companion would
ever be able to half-carry, half-drag him to safety before the
ea got them both.

The last stretch before the steps was all broken rock
underfoot, with rock pools right up to and beneath the
overhang of the cliff.

Suddenly: 'Hey – Johnny – Look over there!'

Pendragon pointed. Close by the cliff, beneath the
overhang, something was poking out of a rock pool: shapeless,
t was, covered with wet rags and shifting limply with every
udge of the encroaching waves. As Steerforth paused to
ollow his companion's pointing finger, he saw that the limb-
ike object terminated in a bare human foot.

'It's a body!' he yelled.

They splashed towards it and saw the humped form lying face down, in the pool, arms and legs trailing grotesquely, th one leg that had betrayed its presence lying awkwardly as broken at the hip, outside the pool.

'Grab a hold!' cried Steerforth, and he took one of th ankles and pulled. The body glided towards him, enabling Pendragon to seize hold of the dead shoulders and turn th body face upwards.

'Cripes!' he exclaimed. 'What the bloody hell? . . .'

Staring sightlessly up at them was the semblance of a goat' head, mouth open to show painted teeth, the imitation fur c the lean cheeks scuffed and torn from being ground agains hard granite. And the whole thing – the masked head – hun brokenly in the water upon a shattered neck.

'Who the hell is it – playing the fool?' demande Pendragon, feeling his sanity slipping away from him.

'Let's have a bloody look and see!' grated his companior And he reached out to pull off the enveloping goat-face mask, revealing a dead, pale face staring up at them bot] with an expression of mild surprise.

'Blimey – it's Doctor Cobb from St Costello – damn' me if ain't!'

The body of the tall and strongly-built man in his early prim was heavy to lift, moreover the dead weight and the saturate clothing added greatly to their burden. The two coastguard men struggled along the cliff's base, now knee deep in water with each incoming wave swamping them to the waist an breaking higher. And the steps still seemed an awful long wa away.

They might have made it with their burden, but Steerfort was caught by a freak wave and slammed against the granit wall, cracking a shoulder agonizingly and causing him t drop his end of the corpse. He cried out in pain, but grope in the swirling water for the dead feet.

'Leave it be, Johnny!' shouted his companion above the ass roar of the sea. 'Go on ahead – I'll carry the bloody thing n me back!' And this he did, hefting the corpse in a fireman's ift across his broad young shoulder, while his older companion lunged on ahead, casting fearful glances back at him.

'You all right, Nick?'

'Yeah – don't hang about!' A wave broke over Pendragon's lead, filling his open mouth, choking him.

Never in his life was Steerforth so relieved as when his hand losed on the rusted iron handrail of the cut steps and he was ble to reach back to assist his companion, just as Pendragon vas inundated once more and the limp burden slipped off his houlder.

'It's going – I can't hold it!' he yelled.

'Let it go – grab hold of my hand!' responded his comrade.

Their hands joined, clasping wrist to wrist, and Pendragon ulled himself to the steps and grabbed at the ironwork.

Both men looked round, to see the body caught in the ackwash of a giant comber which, having smashed into the liff, retreated with all its power and fury still intact, taking he broken body with it; carrying it out to sea, towards the next most westerly headland – on the way to the wild waste of ocean.

At about the same time that the remains of Doctor Tom Cobb were swallowed up forever from the sight of man, one of Wainhouse's young aides, Detective Constable Fred Wright, drove out to Seeley Park Hotel in answer to a call from the manager concerning the police circular about the reporting of guests who had not been seen around for a while.

Seeley Park, built by a Cornish tin-mining magnate in the eighteenth century, had been sold by his descendants after World War II and, following a decade in which it was unsuccessfully operated as a preparatory school and later as a council home for deprived children, was bought up by a nationwide hotel chain and turned into a de luxe, high-priced country club cum time-sharing apartment complex and hotel-restaurant.

Wright was greeted rather offhandedly by the suavely suited resident manager, taken up to the latter's splendid office ensconced in a Chippendale chair and given the information

'We're not *specially* worried about Mr Porchester, you understand, Constable – yes, Porchester's the name – Harold Myles Porchester, of The Towers, Ocean Drive, Sydney Australia. Have you got that?

'Mr Porchester time-shares the Frobisher Suite August through September. Comes over every year. Has his teeth fixed in Harley Street, his suits made in Savile Row – I expect you know the routine, Constable.

'Where in London? Well, he usually stays at his Pall Mall club, that's *The Antipodean* – caters for Australians and New Zealanders mainly, of course. Only, he wasn't going to London when he went away three weeks ago – Thursday it was – but to somewhere in the Cotswolds to start with.

'No, I don't recall the name of the place, but he was calling in to see a gentleman on business, he told me. We had a drink together at the bar before dinner. I remember that he made a particular point of letting drop that the gentleman in question was titled. Tremendously snobbish about titles, the colonials – don't you find?

'Yes, Mr Porchester is unmarried. A bachelor, in fact. Age? – oh, I would say in his mid-forties. Yes, I suppose he wouldn't have taken his passport with him. No car – travels simply *everywhere* by taxi.

'Search the apartment? Will that be necessary, Constable? I mean, I was only responding to your request purely out of a public duty. One couldn't say that Mr Porchester has *gone missing* – it's simply that we had expected him back earlier. Oh, very well – if you insist.

'Mail? – yes, there was one letter that arrived for him, and I have it here. The Royal coat of arms on the flap, and a *very* grand envelope.

'Right away, Constable, I'll take you up to the Frobisher
160

suite myself. No trouble. Oh, but I do beg you to treat this matter with discretion.

'The good name of Seeley Park, you know. And we do so *greatly* contribute to the tourist industry. Invisible export and all that, ha–ha.'

Scotland Yard was officially 'called in' that afternoon, late. Arkwright and Turner flew down to Cornwall by helicopter, arriving on the football ground behind the police station in St Costello, where they were met by the assistant chief constable and his entourage. Wainhouse stood well to the rear and was dismayed to see the warmth with which Arkwright greeted Tina May – they kissed cheeks – and by the DCC's obvious deference to both parties.

After a brief exchange the men from the Yard departed in a patrol car, taking Tina May with them.

'Where are we going, Derek?' she asked.

'To clear the whole thing up,' he replied. 'Like I told Turner here, the answers lie in why that head was brought to Clifftop Cottage in the first place. Today, the answer to the head dropped into our lap. All else will follow – and we're off to set the train in motion.' Nor would he vouchsafe any further explanation, merely contenting himself with the good-natured comment that she – Tina – had done quite enough to solve the mystery of the severed head and all that had followed, and that it was now up to the police in the shape of Scotland Yard to tie up the loose ends.

'And you're being permitted to stick around and see it happen, Tina,' he said. 'Which is a demonstration in itself of the high regard in which you stand with us.' He added with a smile: 'As if you need to be told.'

They came to Trepoll Haven, and the main street was deserted, the holidaymakers and tourists having abandoned the place to the gathering dusk and the chill evening wind that spoke of coming autumn. No one in sight; but many a curtain twitched upon their passing.

161

Past the church of St Botolph, and in through the gate bearing the legend: *Vicarage.*

'This is where it all began,' said Arkwright.

The diminished Wakeley household comprised only the vicar and a living-in maid-of-all-work who answered the door. There was an agency nurse of sharp features and commanding appearance who stood four-square to the unannounced and uninvited visitors and denied their advance, even when Arkwright produced his credentials.

'I don't care who you are, sir,' declared the woman with a cunning approach that was half-way between respect and defiance, 'Doctor Strang's orders were quite specific: the vicar's not to be disturbed by anyone. The poor man is in a very debilitated state and I wouldn't take the responsibility of admitting you without Doctor Strang's approval. And I can't telephone him because he's in Truro today.'

'It will be perfectly in order for us to see Mr Wakeley, Sister,' murmured Arkwright placatingly. 'Doctor May, here, is a fully-qualified physician.'

The woman, who was from out of the district and not aware of Trepoll Haven's distinguished visitor, took a second look at Tina and immediately melted. 'Well, I'm sure that will be all right,' she purred, ogling the TV celebrity in the manner that Tina had come to recognize and shrink away from. 'This way, please.' And she led them upstairs.

The patient was propped up by pillows in a handsome, plainly-carved Victorian four-poster bed. Muffled in dressing gown and woolly scarf, the Honourable Reverend Arthur Wakeley looked like the ghost of a ghost: pale as parchment, emaciated, every bone of his face and hands pitifully revealed beneath stretched skin. Only the eyes behind the pebble glasses were alive, watchful and – thought Tina, remembering Strang's description of the old man's condition – far from betraying signs of mental collapse. The eyes flickered over Tina with a flash of recognition; Wakeley continued to regard her while Arkwright introduced himself and Turner.

'I'm sorry to intrude upon you this way, sir,' he continued, 'but you'll appreciate that we're still pursuing the inquiries into your wife's death, and there is every indication, now, that she was murdered.'

Wakeley inclined his head with a gesture of submission to the vagaries of fate. 'I am inclined to believe, also, that this is so, sir,' he murmured.

'I'd like you to answer a few questions,' said Arkwright, and when Wakeley nodded assent and indicated for them to be seated, he went straight in to the assault: 'When did you last see Mrs Wakeley alive?' he demanded.

'On Sunday evening,' said the other. 'We had a light supper together after I had conducted Evensong. I then went to bed early, leaving my wife to watch television.'

'At what time did she come to bed?'

'I did not hear her retire.'

Arkwright looked down at the sheaf of notes which he had produced from his breast pocket. Tina, with her familiarity of law court manners and the techniques of advocacy, guessed that the gesture was only a cosmetic act to allow him to marshal his thoughts and also keep his adversary in suspense and imbalance. His next question came right out of the blue, and was delivered without him looking up from the paper:

'I think, sir, that you had a visitor on the tenth of this month.' More a statement, really, than a question.

'The – tenth?' The old man's puzzled confusion was genuine, thought Tina.

'That was two weeks ago, Monday,' prompted Arkwright.

'Ah, yes,' said Wakeley. 'I remember now. Yes.'

'Friend of yours, sir?'

'No, no. I had never met him before.'

'Ah, a business call. Someone trying to sell you something, I suppose. Life insurance – a subscription, perhaps?'

'No. It was a private matter, Superintendent.'

'Ah – a private matter.' Arkwright nodded in agreement.

(He's playing with him! thought Tina, who had never seen her friend Derek Arkwright in his role of interrogator before. The experience of watching familiar speech patterns and accustomed facial expressions turned to perverse uses she found curiously disconcerting.)

Presently, Arkwright said: 'If my information is correct, sir, your brother also had a visit from this gentleman.'

Tina distinctly saw the gnarled hands stiffen and clutch at the edge of the bed sheet when the detective made the comment.

'Is it likely, sir?' continued the probe.

'It – it's likely,' came the reply.

'Would this be touching upon the same – private matter?'

'It – it's likely.'

'*Very* likely, wouldn't you say, sir?'

Wakeley gave something that could have been interpreted as a nod, and Arkwright did not repeat the question, but went off at a tangent:

'Your brother – the noble lord – he doesn't resemble you very much, I believe, sir.'

The beginnings of a wry smile touched the corners of the thin lips when the man in the bed replied: 'Even brothers, Mr Arkwright, frequently possess vastly differing personalities.'

'Your brother had this – gentleman – thrown out, didn't he, sir?'

The interjection, delivered in harsh, uncompromising tones, made Tina start with alarm: she had almost forgotten the presence of Detective Sergeant Turner, who had taken a seat slightly behind, and out of her vision.

Without waiting for a reply to his question, Turner threw another:

'Did *you* also kick him out, Mr Wakeley?'

'I – I did no such thing,' faltered the clergyman. 'It would have been – quite against my principles.'

'Of course it would, sir,' agreed Turner. 'You being a man of the Church and all that. As regards your lady wife – I take it that Mrs Wakeley was present at this discussion? . . .'

164

It seemed to Tina that the man in the bed was half-way to framing a denial; but he finally nodded.

'What was Mrs Wakeley's reaction to the gentleman, sir?'

It was then that Tina saw a return of the expression that she had discerned in Wakeley's face when first she had met him on the beach: the expression of dreadful fear.

He did not reply to Turner's question.

The seeming eternity of a whole half-minute must have ticked slowly past before Derek Arkwright intervened upon the silence:

'Mr Wakeley, I don't want to insult you,' he said, 'but we are dealing with a serious matter, a matter of life and death. Personal feelings, normal politenesses, have to go by the board in such circumstances as these, you understand?'

A barely imperceptible nod from his addressee, and Arkwright continued: 'Now, without offence, I can point out, can I not, that your wife was many years your junior?'

'That is so.'

'An attractive woman. A vivacious, life-loving – perhaps some might have thought a pleasure-loving woman. Again, I am not trying deliberately to be rude to you, sir, but scarcely the type whom one would expect to be married to a country parson who was more than old enough to be her father. Do you take my point?'

Wakeley took his point, all right – and bowed his head in meek acquiescence of a harsh and unarguable fact that he must have had his nose rubbed into many times in innumerable whispered 'asides'.

'It must have been thought,' continued Arkwright relentlessly, 'that such a woman would only have contracted such a marriage for money. But, as I am given to understand, Mrs Wakeley had ample means of her own. Is this correct?'

'My wife received a considerable inheritance from her father,' came the reply in a dying voice of despair.

'Yes. The father was Sam Hardacre, a scrap-metal merchant,' said Arkwright. 'Came out of the army after the war with nothing but his gratuity – and made himself into a millionaire by the time he was thirty. In the course of which he served two prison sentences for fraud. But nobody's perfect.

'The whole point I'm trying to make, Mr Wakeley, is that Sam Hardacre's daughter had not the slightest need or call to marry an aged country parson who had nothing to live on but his stipend, plus a small inheritance which, as the younger son, he had from his father.'

'*True?*'

Tina winced at the spare brutality of the demand.

The thin hands plucked at the edge of the bed sheet.

'My wife – she anticipated certain – other advantages,' whispered Wakeley.

'Ah!' Derek Arkwright exhaled in what almost a sigh of relief. 'At last we've come to the nub of the matter,' he said. And he extracted a sheet of paper from the pile on his lap. The man in the bed watched him doing so with an expression of growing unease, licking his thin lips, his eyes shadowed with foreboding.

'I have here,' said Arkwright, in a bright, 'now, let's get down to business' sort of voice which was in sharp contrast to the oblique and insinuating manner with which he had conducted the interview thus far, 'I have here a letter addressed to a certain Harold M. Porchester at The Antipodean Club, Pall Mall, London, SW1. The letter was found in the suite which belongs to the addressee at the Seeley Park Hotel, Seeley, Cornwall. It is from a solid-sounding enterprise called The Heritage Genealogical Society, of Park Lane, Mayfair, and reads as follows:

'"Dear Sir, Further to our last communication, we now enclose herewith the genealogical tree of the Porchester and Charters families, duly engrossed and illuminated. The present writer has made further inquiries of the West Riding County Records and confirmed that Lucinda Charters and David Arthur Porchester were indeed married in the rite of the Roman Catholic Church in September 1883, so that their issue Charles Martin Porchester – killed in action 1917 – was indeed the rightful 5th Baron Porchester, and that the present

166

incumbent James Francis Wakeley, born 1900, has no right to the title of 6th Baron.

'"We can, without hesitation, urge you to lodge your rightful claim, as grandson of the said Charles Martin Porchester, with The College of Heralds, in the complete confidence that your claim will be upheld, that the said James Francis Wakeley and his heirs and descendants"' – (it was at this point that Arkwright looked up from the paper and gave the man in the bed a significant glance) – '"*his heirs and descendants will be excluded* – and that you will be confirmed in your true rank and style as 6th Baron Porchester.

'"Yours faithfully, et cetera, et cetera." And that, Mr Wakeley,' concluded Arkwright, 'is the letter which got Porchester thrown out of your brother's house for his pains, the gist of which he then quoted to you, verbatim, to get your reaction.

'What *was* your reaction, sir?'

It seemed to Tina that Arthur Wakeley (surely, by the burden of the letter, no longer 'the Honourable', though still 'Reverend') had further shrunk in content, so that his skeletal basis was overlaid only with a fine patina of skin; but if the corporeal tissues had diminished, the eyes behind the magnifying lenses had grown even larger, more staring.

'I told Porchester,' he said at length, 'that it was in his own interest to make his claim with the College of Heralds, that I could not be a party – notwithstanding my brother's view of the matter – to the suppression of truth. Earthly titles having no power to seduce me, and the prospect of succeeding to the barony upon my older brother's death – he being a bachelor – is not of the slightest interest.'

'But that wasn't your wife's reaction, was it?' said Arkwright.

Wakeley's last declaration had been delivered with a commendable firmness, and a sincerity which certainly rang true with at least one of his hearers; his next answer, when it

167

came – and it was slow in coming – carried the hollow ring of counterfeit coin.

'My wife had no opinion to give!' he cried. 'As a woman, she was not concerned with matters of succession – that is a man's business. . . .'

'Porchester went away from here,' said Arkwright, 'and was expected back at the Seeley Park Hotel. He has not been seen since leaving this house.'

'My wife had a certain foolishness about the title!' babbled Wakeley. 'Almost an obsession. It was on account of her humble origins, you see. . . .'

'On the Saturday following Porchester's disappearance,' interposed Arkwright, 'a severed head was delivered at Clifftop Cottage.'

'Many times I begged her to put away the folly of pride,' wailed the man in the bed. 'I quoted the Scriptures, telling her that "*Pride goeth before destruction*" – Proverbs sixteen, verse eighteen.'

'That head,' said Arkwright, 'lost, yet found again, has now been established beyond doubt, from dental evidence, as being that of Harold M. Porchester.

'What do you make of that, Mr Wakeley?'

The clergyman choked in the middle of trying to assemble a reply, and flailed the air with his skinny hands and arms, as if fighting the very elements for breath. Tina rushed across to him, swiftly searching in neglected store rooms of her mind for the procedure she had been taught to follow in cases of seizure.

The Written Statement of Mr Leonard Jordan, of Riverside Cottage, Trepoll Haven, Cornwall. Given on today's date.

This statement is given by me of my own free will, having been cautioned as to my rights by Detective Sergeant A.W. Turner.

I am an orphan, my mother having died at my birth and I was brain damaged, Doctor Strang having messed me up. They say he squashed my head with his instrument or something and that's why I sometimes get bad headaches and forget things.

I admit I was a member of the so-called coven formed by the late Mr Ellis Duke. Others included Mrs Glenda Wakeley and Doctor Thomas Oliver Cobb, at least Cobb was a member till Duke died. He was very ashamed of being a member, I think, and persuaded Duke to mask out our faces in the pictures that Duke painted in his bathroom for fear he'd be identified and ruin his career. When Duke died, he gave up the coven, being ashamed to mingle with us common folk. Mrs Wakeley, she wasn't so stuck up and stayed. I took over leadership from Ellis Duke.

I would have done anything for Glenda Wakeley. We was lovers till her death. On the evening of the 20th instant she sent for me and said that she had a dead body on her hands which must be got rid of or she would be blamed for his death. I had been a butcher's apprentice so it was no trouble to cut up the body and put it in Glenda's deep freeze, her idea than was for me to burn it

/To D.S. Turner of New Scotland Yard.

/Doctor Strang broadly confirms this, but with reservations as to his culpability.

/See also statement of Ms Meg Chambers.

/at Messrs. Saint-

/Continued . . .

piece by piece in the solid fuel stove at Clifftop Cottage by night so no one would see the smoke. Glenda had a key of the cottage.

On the Saturday Glenda delivers the last part of the body to be burnt, which was the head. This she leaves at the cottage by arrangement. When I arrive to burn it, I see Doctor May coming back with PC Bert Tuttle, and only manage to get away with the head in time. We did not know that Doctor May had rented the cottage from Doctor Heymans.

Sunday evening Glenda sends for me. Says she's seen Doctor May and she won't make any trouble. She then tells me that she's finished with me. We have a quarrel and I hit her. She falls and hits her head unconscious. I leave her lying there.

Monday morning I go to work at the North Park Holiday Camp. Imagine how I feel when I find Glenda lying in the pool and I know she committed suicide because of me. I think she came to her senses and realized how she'd broken my heart. It was remorse what done for her.

I still tell myself I might have brought her round if that Doctor May woman hadn't stuck her oar in and insisted that Glenda was past all help. For this I hate that woman. And I swore I'd get my own back on her.

For Glenda's sake, I go on covering up for her. The head I burn in the open fire grate at my place even though the neighbours

ley's ab-
batoir,
St
Costello.

For the
record,
not
rented,
but
loaned.

/Mrs
Wake-
ley's
death

/Continued . . .

complain of the smell and it doesn't all burn away so I have to bury the skull in the garden.

Yes I admit I gave Doctor May plenty of harassment. This is because I figure she must be a White Witch like Doctor Heymans what drove Ellis Duke to kill himself. Why else as soon as she turns up does everything bad start to happen? I told the coven she'd been sent by Doctor Heymans to smash the coven. They was all against her when I told them this. When Mrs Penlee told me Doctor May was scared of snakes I puts an adder through her door like I once did to Doctor Strang for messing me up at birth.

Finally I'm glad I did what I did. For Glenda's sake I would do it all over again. I loved that woman.

(signed)

Later:
I have been shown a passport photograph of a man named Harold M. Porchester, and I declare that this is the man whose body I butchered and whose head I took from Clifftop Cottage, then burnt and buried.

(signed)

due to drowning in early hours of Monday a.m. (Joint p.m. report – q.v.)

/Confirmed by Doctor May's statement. (q.v.)

Eleven

In the event, the departure of Tina May from Trepoll Haven was very low key. She tried to ring Heymans and inform him, out of courtesy, of her intent: he was not available to speak to her. She left early the following morning with Arkwright and Turner, who, bowing to her dislike of flying, abandoned the idea of going back to London by helicopter in favour of a comfortable drive in a chauffeured police limosine – not by the motorway, but by the scenic route through rural Cornwall, Devon, Somerset, Dorset, Wiltshire, Hampshire and on. About two hundred and fifty miles.

She had half a notion to make a gesture of farewell to Lucius Strang, but for some reason which she never explained to herself she decided not to. Only Detective Inspector Wainhouse was there to see them off; the man's lugubrious gaze haunted Tina from the background; it was as if he wanted to offer something – an apology, a word of regret, perhaps – but he never got around to it.

The big car wound down the valley road, so recently in the grip of the river, no longer murderous but slow-moving, slight and serene; it debouched into the busy traffic of St Costello and took the eastbound road out of town. They chanced to pass by the end of the road where the Cobbs' silent Edwardian mansion stood, its windows eyeless and shuttered in mourning. Tina shuddered to see it.

Through the gently undulating countryside on the way to Plymouth, they sat together in silence, all with their own thoughts. The implications of Lenny Jordan's 'confession' had given all three of them much material for speculation and conjecture: it was Tina who brought the issues to a point:

172

'What will happen to Lenny?'

'He's been charged as an accessory after the act,' replied Arkwright, who was sitting on her left, with Turner on her right. 'And the act is murder.'

'Will he get a long sentence, Derek?'

'If found guilty,' said Arkwright, 'and he certainly will be, he might get away with a fairly short stretch on the grounds of diminished responsibility. It would depend upon a medical report.'

'His statement's quite coherent,' said Tina. 'How much of it was his own, and by how much did you have to help and prompt him, Sergeant Turner?'

Turner looked a little huffy at this. 'I did no more than try to help him clarify his thoughts,' he said. 'While retaining his characteristic mode of expression,' he added.

Tina nodded, and there the discussion languished for a while. It was Arkwright who set it afoot again:

'I have my own theory about how and why Glenda Wakeley killed Porchester,' he said, adding: 'I take it, for the purposes of this conversation, that the fact of her having murdered Porchester is common ground?'

The question hung in the air for only a few moments.

'Undoubtedly, I would say,' responded Turner.

'It's a reasonable premise,' conceded Tina. 'And the most likely.'

'The manner, the method, of the killing I'd like to leave aside for a while,' said Arkwright. 'Let's get her motives straight. She was obsessed about the title, enough to kill for it. A bit over the top, you think? Believe me, I've come across guys - and dolls - who'd sell their souls, over and over again, for a handle to their name. And do.'

Tina nodded. 'Old Wakeley put his finger on it,' she said, 'when he lost control and went on about her "foolishness" over the title, which he put down to a reaction from what he called her humble origins. That makes sense to me. She was an obsessive social climber.'

'Fair enough,' interposed Turner, 'But she mucked in with

the coven and they were a pretty mixed bunch – small shopkeepers, a village copper, not to mention Lenny. Does that sound like social climbing?'

Arkwright looked doubtful, but Tina chipped in firmly:

'*Nostalgie de la boue!*' she said. 'That's what it was with Glenda – just that.'

'Come again, Doctor?' responded Turner.

'What the French call nostalgia for the mud,' said Tina. 'And it's confined to people who've outgrown their own egos. The more puffed-up the ego, the more they fall for *nostalgie de la boue*. Call it slumming. Multi-millionaires who wear their threadbare coat cuffs as a badge of honour have it, Queen Marie Antoinette with her satin-clad milkmaids and shepherds playing at being peasants had it. Glenda went in for slumming with the coven to throw into sharper perspective her position as an Honourable and a Ladyship-elect.'

'I'll buy that,' said Arkwright, looking relieved. 'Since it helps my hypothesis along.'

They came to the River Tamar, forming the boundary between the duchy of Cornwall and the county of Devon. Beyond the massive toll bridge lay what all good Cornishmen call 'furrin parts'. Plymouth was just across the water, and Turner, born and bred a Plymouth man, was full of anecdotal information about the famous city and naval base. He insisted that they should take time out to drive up to the Hoe. And this brought a natural break to their discussion.

The Hoe was certainly breathtaking. To the west, wooded slopes swept grandly down to the water's edge; eastwards looked craggy, twentieth-century and functional; Drake's island was placed so dramatically off-centre of the broad canvas of the wonderful natural harbour that to shift it a yard would have completely upset the balance of the composition.

Their driver had gone for a walk along the promenade to stretch her legs. The three passengers were relaxing in the back of the limousine.

'Which brings us to Cobb,' said Arkwright, 'and now we really *are* in the field of speculation.

'He made no statement. Owned no diary – so far as we've been able to find. Confided in no one. So what do we know, what can we reasonably speculate, about his movements?

'Let's go back to Glenda. She killed Porchester to ensure that her husband succeeded to the title and the stately home – a not unreasonable hope, because her husband's brother is ten years his senior and suffering from heart disease. She wants a quick, certain method of killing the only man standing in the way of her expectations.

'Where did she go to get it?' He looked at them both for answer.

'To Cobb,' responded Tina. 'And that presupposes that he – as well as Lenny – was her lover. And by her own admissions on the only occasion that I met her, two men at a time would be quite within her style.'

'So Cobb provides the – well, we'll assume it's poison,' said Arkwright. 'And Lenny's on hand to dispose of the body. She's got a tidy set-up, right?'

'Better than that, sir,' responded Turner. 'She's got it so well organized that Lenny is totally unaware of Cobb's part in the proceedings. Lenny's statement doesn't in any way implicate him in Mrs Wakeley's crime. If Cobb was also her lover, Lenny almost certainly didn't know about it.'

'He couldn't have,' concurred Tina. 'Or he'd have shouted it from the rooftops, let alone incriminated Cobb in his statement. When a man's so obsessed with a woman as to do for her what he did for Glenda, jealousy's never very far away.'

Arkwright nodded pleasurably. 'Glad to hear you both say it,' he remarked. 'It all goes to strengthen my hypothesis. And do you know what happens next in my hypothesis?'

Again, he gave them both a searching glance. It was Tina who snapped a finger and thumb, eyes shining with enlightenment.

'Having disposed of the one impediment to her heart's
175

desire – discounting his lordship, who's going to die soon anyhow,' she said, 'I reckon that Glenda decided to tidy up her life by separately giving her two current lovers their marching orders.'

'Very good,' said Arkwright. 'And which one does she dismiss first?'

'Well,' said Tina, 'if I've guessed aright about your hypothesis, it has to be Cobb.'

'Very good again!' repeated Arkwright.

'I don't get it,' said Turner glumly.

'Here comes the driver,' said Arkwright, 'and about time too, if we're to get to Salisbury in time for lunch.'

Through Devon, past Exeter cathedral's towers rising above the old city; onwards, hugging the coast, with tantalizing glimpses of the wide blue sea. Somerset, Dorset and the Vale of Blackmoor.

'She undoubtedly sent Cobb packing first,' said Arkwright. 'Next came Lenny, who still had the job of finding another means to get rid of the tell-tale skull. For reasons best known to herself, Tina, she'd decided you were not going to make any trouble over the skull – so she quite brutally told Lenny they were all washed up. A dangerous pastime, raising the fury of powerful, mentally deprived men like Lenny. In his fury, he hit out at her, scarcely knowing his own strength. But he was bright enough to know that she was only unconscious – that he hadn't killed her.'

'And then,' interposed Tina, 'Cobb came back again.'

'He had to, didn't he?' said Arkwright. 'Or the scenario doesn't hang together. He came back to plead with her – also remembering that he had laid his career on the line by supplying her with a fatal dose of poison – or so we reckon. Maybe he wanted assurances of her future silence, to cover up for him even if she were found out.'

'I'm with you now, sir,' said Turner. 'Her assurances of silence, his hope that she would cover up for him no matter

176

what – they were all lying there, helpless, in front of him.'

'It works,' said Arkwright. 'He dresses her in the swimsuit and mackintosh. Takes her in her car, still unconscious – and lowers her quietly into the empty pool, in the deserted, early-morning, sleeping camp.'

'I ad-libbed it to him,' breathed Tina. 'We discussed it just like that, and he agreed with me. In his surgery. The first time we met.' She shuddered in the certain knowledge that someone had walked over her grave-to-be. 'Poor, foolish Glenda. She played every card in her hand – and still she lost out.'

'There's a double irony here,' said Arkwright, and he took a letter from out of his briefcase. 'This is from the College of Heralds, and it's in reply to a communication from Porchester. He'd written to them, you see, before he ever called upon the Wakeley brothers. It's a very impressive document, redolent of authority lightly borne, and utterly unimpeachable. I'll read you the most relevant passage. It's addressed to the applicant, Porchester.

'It says: "Notwithstanding the contention of the organiz-ation calling itself The Heritage Genealogical Society, the issue of the supposed marriage between Lucinda Charters and David Arthur Porchester was thoroughly investigated when the question of the succession to the 5th Barony was disputed by your forebears in 1923 and it was established that no such marriage took place and that Charles Martin Porchester was a bastard. You therefore have no claim to the title. Yours" – et cetera.'

'So Glenda had nothing to fear after all!' exclaimed Tina. 'She killed – and was killed – for nothing. Nothing at all.'

'You could extend similar sympathy to Porchester,' said Arkwright. 'This letter was waiting for him back at the Seeley Park Hotel. If he'd called in there before going off down to beard the Wakeleys in Trepoll Haven, he'd have given up the whole thing – *and still be alive now!*'

*

'On the face of it, Cobb should have encountered no trouble at all,' said Arkwright. 'He knew he'd be performing the post mortem on her. He could have fudged the issue of the defensive bruises she received from Lenny. The inside-out swimsuit, of course, he knew nothing about. Nobody spotted it but you, Tina.'

'Wainhouse knew!' interjected Tina. 'I told him, and he laughed me to scorn. I was furious – furious!'

'He also told Cobb,' said Arkwright slowly and with a heavy portentousness.

'How do you know that – did he tell you?' asked Tina.

'Only when I asked him,' replied the other. 'And you can be sure he mentioned it to Cobb in a scoffing, "what else can you expect from an hysterical little woman" manner. But Cobb took it seriously – oh, yes! That and you having seen the defensive bruises too. And no doubt formed your own opinion on both points.'

Tina stared at him. 'But you don't think that – just because of that, he? . . .'

'If we're taking my hypothesis this far, still, it's the only answer that fits,' said Arkwright.

'Nancy Chambers kept her taxi in a quiet lane behind her cottage,' supplied Turner. He gave his chief a shrewd admiring glance. 'I wondered why you got me to check it out, Mr Arkwright.'

'When you made the appointment to call and see him, he went to Trepoll by the back roads,' said Arkwright. 'No one saw him turn that taxi into a death trap by removing and loosening the wheel nuts. It was a ploy worth trying – and it nearly succeeded, give or take a quarter of a mile or so.'

'Nancy was going to tell me something,' said Tina. 'Even while she was dying, she tried to communicate.'

'The very existence of a witch's coven in a closed society like Trepoll Haven must have generated a lot of gossip among the locals who weren't members,' said Arkwright. 'And mostly of the speculative, seamy kind, I should guess. It's probable that Nancy had a few spicy gobbets to pass on to you maybe involving Cobb, even if she didn't know it. It's possible that he wasn't too disappointed with his mobile death trap, after all.'

'Another thing about her,' said Tina. 'When I – that's to say Cobb and I – did the post mortem on her, we found the letters DD tattooed under her armpit. I don't know if Cobb put it in the p.m. report, or if it was followed up. . . .'

'The sister became very cooperative after she'd got over the first shock of Nancy's death,' said Arkwright. 'Yes, the DD tattoo was in the report and we questioned her about it.'

'And? . . .'

'It seems that, for all the probity of her mature years, the young Nancy was quite a tearaway in her teens,' said Arkwright. 'She'd been a groupie with a fifties motorbike gang called the Dirty Devils. And they all carried the DD initials.

'What kids will get up to!

'Driver! Is that the spire of Salisbury cathedral I see up ahead?'

'Yes, sir,' replied the WPC chauffeur, who had been listening to the foregoing conversation with such absorbed interest as to put her driving at fault.

Replete after a magnificent luncheon of saddle of lamb in the cathedral city's most famous hostelry, the three of them sat in the quiet of the spacious walled Close, in the very shadow of the highest church spire in England, a shadow that had moved around the scissor-cut grass of the Close, at the dictates of the sun, for six hundred years. They fed crumbs to a quartette of cheeky jackdaws. A couple of boy choristers in black cassocks walked past them towards a side door of the great edifice, both blowing bubble gum.

'At this stage,' said Arkwright, 'my hypothesis dictates that Cobb's intention was directed towards concealing his affair with Glenda and her entire involvement with the murder of Porchester. This would put him in the clear, both as regards

179

his supplying her with the poison and his murdering her. think he then had a brainwave. Why not sell everyone the idea that the head which Tina May claimed to have seen was that of Ellis Duke, whose body was providentially swallowed up by the Atlantic eight months before?

'It was a not-outrageous supposition. Turner, here, was very sold on the idea. Quite independently. And more or les convinced me. True, Turner?'

'Very true, sir,' admitted the other. 'It was a good theory then, and it's still a good theory in essence.'

'There was one big snag, still, in making the idea stick,' said Arkwright.

'*Me!*' interjected Tina May.

'Right.'

'I alone had seen and could identify the head from any good photo that was found and presented to me,' she said 'Therefore, to make the Ellis Duke idea stick – *I had to be go rid of!*'

Both men looked at her – and with the odd, sidelong glance – half pitying, half abhorrent – which people reserve for the wretched survivors of particularly horrendous disasters.

She took a deep breath and said – for it had to be said and she had to work through it, to exorcise the memory: 'He invited me to a picnic on Dorwell Head. His mother had made up the tea hamper. We talked of this and that. About his mother. About why I went in for pathology. And then he brought the subject round to the severed head. He quizzed me closely as to what I'd noticed about it. And then – I let drop about my connection with Scotland Yard. I spoke about you, Derek. By this time, I had become thoroughly convinced of the possibility that the head might have been that of Ellis Duke.

'In fact, at his suggestion, I said I'd ring you immediately I got back to the cottage and put the idea to you.

'And I suppose, because of that. . . .'

She stared first at Arkwright, then at Turner – then back again to Arkwright. Both men created the image in her mind of what it would be like to rise from the dead and appear to one's friends.

'But for that,' she whispered, 'but for the use I could have been to him, to put the idea to you, he would have done what he'd brought me up Dorwell Head to do!'

Arkwright nodded – and she had a vision of herself and the murderer standing on the cliff edge, side by side, looking down at the black fangs of granite two hundred feet below.

Like the resolving of a complex Chinese puzzle, the last piece then fell neatly into place, the ease and inevitability with which it fitted there proving beyond all argument that there was no other possible solution to the seemingly inexplicable events at Trepoll Haven – and that Arkwright's indictment against Doctor Thomas O. Cobb was a true bill.

For, as Tina then said: 'But when I wasn't able to reach you that night when the storm began, Derek, and I remembered the very specific dental evidence I'd noticed in the severed head, I rang and told Cobb about it.'

'That completely ditched his plan,' said Arkwright, 'for he would have known, of course, that Duke wore dentures in the upper front. His severed head theory was completely out of court, along with any hope of pointing the finger of suspicion at Lenny, as Duke's murderer – undoubtedly his next move.

'And so, Tina, he came after you again. . . .'

He came after me again. . . .

On a night of storm, wearing that terrifying mask. To silence me for good. Only, he missed me in the dark and went blundering off along the clifftop till he lost his way and fell over the edge.

The man who confessed that he was scared silly of heights.

Twelve

Autumn had come to Lochiel Street. The trees had mos
unseasonably begun to shed their russet leaves and, lik
parasols with holes in, were making dappled sun-spots i
their shadows on the pavement. The evening paper had bee
delivered to Number 18 and was still stuck, half in and ha
out of the letter box; Tina collected it on the way inside.

'Tina!' Maggie came running at the sound of her key in th
lock. 'How lovely to see you – but I hadn't expected you bac
till late.'

'Derek Arkwright offered me dinner,' said Tina, 'but, yo
know? – all I wanted was to slump down in my own armchai
in my own home. How are you, Maggie?'

Maggie was great – and looking great. Her superbly
proportioned figure had plumped out a little, and this wa
probably due to her symptomatic new passion for gooe
cakes. 'You look marvellous, Tina,' she said with a certai
wistful envy. Me, I can't get into any of my skirts already.

'It couldn't have been my rest cure,' said Tina wryly. 'But
oddly – I do feel pretty good, and I'm sleeping like a top
Have been for the last couple of nights, anyhow. Any news

'Oh, hello You.' The enormous cat ambled up to he
rubbed his great head against her ankle, collected his rightfu
due of a tickle behind the ear, and preceded her towards th
kitchen with his mincing, androgynous little steps.

'No news,' said Maggie, 'except that Simon Elles wa
ringing you all day yesterday and again today. Begged me t
give him your Cornwall number, but I stone-walled. He'll b
on again this evening, I shouldn't wonder.

'Like a cup of tea?'

'Please. Lead me to it!'

She settled herself down in her favourite wicker armchair in the bright and airy kitchen to which the pair of them so often gravitated. You the cat pranced on to her lap with surprising lightness.

'Tell me how it all worked out, down in Trepoll Haven,' demanded Maggie, putting the kettle on. 'By the way, you have eaten?'

'Had a tremendous luncheon in Salisbury. What happened in Trepoll Haven's a long story and it will have to wait. How have you been getting along? Anything from Jock?'

'He sent me a postcard from Sydney, telling me that all was well and that he and his partner were flying out to their island,' said Maggie. 'It arrived the day before yesterday and took weeks to get here. What do you think to? . . .'

Tina was never called upon to answer whatever her question was, for the phone rang at her elbow. She brushed You off her lap and reached out to pick it up.

'Is that Doctor May's residence? Mr Elles's secretary here. Mr Elles would like to speak to Doctor May if she's available. She is? Hold the line, please.'

There was what promised to be an interminable wait, and Tina's eye strayed to the evening paper which had been resting on her lap underneath the cat. She registered one of the sub-headlines on the front page:

REMAND PRISONER HANGED IN CELL

'Hello, Tina! So you're back?'

'Yes, Simon, I'm back. Back for good. And I hope never to see Trepoll Haven again.'

'So *that's* where you were. Wish you'd told me. I've got a godfather in St Costello who's quite a giddy old playboy for his age. He'd have been delighted to wine and dine you. However. . . .

'Tina, I've got news for you. Really quite wonderful news. You'll remember I wrote telling you that we – that's to say the board – had decided to put back the new series of *Pathologist* till the New Year? Well, my dear! At the first *whisper* of it in

183

the press there was such an outcry from your many fans – a veritable public outcry – that we've – that's to say the board's reconsidered, and. . . .'

She had the message in the first few phrases; the rest was going to be Simon Elles exculpating himself as well as he was able from any suspicion that he had played any part in trying to fade out the show. She let him ramble on, giving him only half an ear, while she glanced down the column that had taken her attention. She read it with mounting interest – and with shocked awareness when a name sprang out at her from the printed page:

> . . . *arrested and held on remand by the magistrates pending trial for murder at the Old Bailey, was found dead in his cell yesterday evening. The police say that he took his own life and no question of foul play arises. James Holmes was accused of murdering his common-law wife Angela Stewart, but had strenuously denied the charge. . . .*

'Are you there, Tina?'

'Yes, I'm sorry – um – Simon. You were saying?'

'Well, that we all couldn't be more happy, and there'll be no question of revamping any of the programmes – no way. Who's to argue with the great British public – not to mention overseas sales? What's the Latin tag? – *Vox populi, vox Dei,* ha–ha. . . .'

> *It is understood that Holmes left a note behind, in which he reiterated his innocence. A Home Office inquiry is to be. . . .*

'Isn't that just marvellous, Tina? Aren't you pleased?'

'Yes, I'm absolutely delighted, Simon. Thanks so much for telling me. It's quite made my day.'

(Dead. Holmes is dead. Guilty or innocent, if I hadn't been quite so bright and pushy in reporting the cut on the woman's hand, he'd still be alive now.

But, then – *she'd* still be dead. . . .)

'Tina? . . .'

184

'Yes, Simon? Sorry.'

'Will you have lunch with me soon. This week?'

'Of course, Simon. Thank you, that will be lovely.'

(What was it the man said? 'The show must go on. . . .')

That, the first night back in her own bed, she slept as she had not slept since – oh, how long she simply couldn't remember; a fulfilment of the promise that she had enjoyed in her last couple of nights in Trepoll Haven, when Derek Arkwright and Sergeant Turner had come down to lift some – most – of the intolerable burden of doubt and fear from her shoulders. She woke to an autumnal morning that had a bite to it, and looked out of her back bedroom window over the quiet gardens of secret Chelsea. There was no one about. Only You the cat, who was making heavy weather of stalking a blackbird who was breakfasting off a snail down by the goldfish pond. Tina had an impulse to warn the blackbird of his imminent peril, but had difficulty in raising the window sash to call out and wreck You's stalk. She need not have bothered; the bird, who must have been well aware of his would-be executioner, took flight long before the big cat came within leaping distance, and You merely turned and minced away for all the world as if mayhem had never entered his head. The incident curiously lightened Tina's spirits which, though well short of euphoria (which she always regarded with suspicion), were already bounding free.

In her shower she rationalized her feelings. Heymans had been right: the change of scenery, the distancing of herself from the day-to-day pressures of her extremely full life, had been beneficial, the rude awakenings of Trepoll Haven no more than a protracted shot of adrenaline that had stirred her to responses and reactions which she had left lying dormant for far too long.

Free-wheeling – that was what she had been doing: the phrase was one of Johnny Kettle's. Life had been too bland, too easy. Just as she had closed her mind to the sharpness of

185

Johnny's death, so had she constructed a carapace about her feelings to everything: to her TV success, which she had come to find something of a bore; to the poor dead folk whom she had let through her hands with no thought for what they might have been, dreamed, suffered, enjoyed. And the same could be said of her self-regarding: how long had it been since she had shaken off the tough-egg image of Tina the Corpse Doctor and had a damned good cry?

Correction: innocent or guilty, the wretched Holmes had won her pity and it had not been of the mawkish kind, but a real regret for the painfully inevitable, and an acceptance of her own part in it as a scientist whose only duty is to seek out, and record, the images of truth.

She dressed herself for all weathers, put on a brave lipstick and went down to breakfast. She had scarcely reached the bottom of the stairs when there came a knock on the door. It was the postman, not the regular one, but a bearer of a special delivery – in this case a wire.

'You open it, Tina.' Maggie hated telegrams.

'No – you. It is addressed to you, after all. If I do it I might put a hex on the wretched thing.'

Maggie opened it the way a cat approaches a bowl of cream: slowly, suspiciously, and with much caution. Her reaction, when she read it, was all bad.

'Oh, my God!'

'Give it to me,' said Tina grimly.

MAGGIE WAINWRIGHT
18 LOCHIEL STREET
CHELSEA LONDON SW3

ENTERPRISE FALLEN APART OWING TO PARTNER HAVING DECAMPED WITH CAPITAL STOP AM WORKING IN BAR TO RAISE FARE MONEY HOME STOP EXPECT ME END OF MONTH STOP TELL TINA

= JOCK

The telegram fell from her fingers and described a gentle

light path towards the hearthrug, chased by You.

She and Maggie stared at each other for a few moments in wild surmise. And then fell into each other's arms, consumed by mutual, uncontrollable laughter.

Tina made a purchase at the tobacconist's on the corner of Lochiel Street and hailed a taxi, directing the driver to take her to Kensal Green.

She had never set foot in the cemetery, nor been within miles of the place, since she and Jeremy Cook had attended Johnny's funeral together; though she had often speculated upon her reactions to the possibility of having to conduct an exhumation there. She paid off the cab and walked to the Garden of Remembrance where, so a kindly attendant had told her, Johnny's ashes would have been strewn among the rose bushes. For a modest fee, he had also informed her, she could have a bush planted there, with the name and dates of the deceased on a small plaque. She had given it some thought, but had finally come down against the idea because Johnny had not only been indifferent to, but sometimes actively hostile to flowers of all kinds; at least, he had always insisted on them being removed from a restaurant table.

No flowers, then; for this special occasion, she had another tribute in mind. . . .

There was a gardener, an oldish fellow in overalls, weeding between the bushes. He nodded affably to Tina and she sensed that she had found the sort of character she needed.

She gave a small cough. 'Hem! Excuse me, but do you like cigars?'

He was bright; went along with her caprice without acting dumb. 'When I can get 'em, lady,' he said. 'Christmas, birthdays and the like. Yes, if you're doing some kind of survey, you can put me down as a cigar smoker who can't afford 'em. Not the good ones. Not the real thing.'

She took from her bag the large cigar that she had bought from the corner shop.

'Is this the kind of thing?' she asked. 'I particularly asked for a Havana. A corona-corona.'

He took the proffered cigar; rolled it between his fingers, shook it close to his ear, sniffed at it appreciatively.

'This here's the real McCoy,' he pronounced.

'You can have it,' said Tina. 'Only – I should like you to smoke it now. Not necessarily all of it, not all at once. And here.' She pointed to a park bench that stood close by the Garden of Remembrance.

'No sooner said than done, lady,' declared her new friend. The pair of them sat down together and he went through a protracted ritual of lighting the big cigar with a match; first warming it in the flame, and then drawing out a luxuriant lungful, which he slowly exhaled.

'Perfection!' he said.

'It's for a friend of mine,' explained Tina. 'His ashes were strewn here. He didn't much care for flowers, but he had a cigar every night after dinner. It was his greatest delight. He used to say that a woman's a woman, but a good cigar's a smoke. He wasn't the first to say it. For as long as I live, I shall never forget the scent of his cigar.'

'Like this, was it?'

'Just like that.'

He smoked in silence for a while, and the delicate aroma drifted over the garden. Presently, he took the cigar out of his mouth. 'If you don't mind,' he said, 'I'll nip off the end and save the rest till I've had me midday snap, if that's all right with you.'

'Yes, that'll be fine.'

'I'll smoke it right here.'

'Good.'

They said goodbye, and Tina was glad that the man had not appeared to recognize her from the TV. Reaching the cemetery gates, she looked back and smiled.

'So long, Johnny,' she murmured.

188